AGOSTINO

ALBERTO MORAVIA (1907–1990), the child of a wealthy family, was raised at home because of illness. He published his first novel, *The Time of Indifference*, at the age of twenty-three. Banned from publishing under Mussolini, he emerged after World War II as one of the most admired and influential of twentieth-century Italian writers. In addition to *Agostino*, New York Review Classics publishes Moravia's novels *Boredom* and *Contempt*.

MICHAEL F. MOORE is the chair of the PEN/Heim Translation Fund. His translations from the Italian include, most recently, *Live Bait* by Fabio Genovesi, *The Drowned and the Saved* by Primo Levi, and *Quiet Chaos* by Sandro Veronesi. He is currently working on a new translation of the nineteenth-century classic *The Betrothed* by Alessandro Manzoni.

D1403509

AGOSTINO

ALBERTO MORAVIA

Translated from the Italian by
MICHAEL F. MOORE

NEW YORK REVIEW BOOKS

New York

THIS IS A NEW YORK REVIEW BOOK
PUBLISHED BY THE NEW YORK REVIEW OF BOOKS
435 Hudson Street, New York, NY 10014
www.nyrb.com

Agostino was first published in Italy in 1945 by Casa editrice Valentino
Bompiani & C. S.p.A.

Library of Congress Cataloging-in-Publication Data
Moravia, Alberto, 1907–1990.
 Agostino / Alberto Moravia ; translated by Michael F. Moore.
    pages cm. — (New York Review Books Classics)
 ISBN 978-1-59017-723-5 (paperback)
 I. Moore, Michael, 1954 August 24– II. Title.
 PQ4829.O62A6313 2014
 853'.912—dc23

                    2013050863

ISBN 978-1-59017-723-5
Available as an electronic book; ISBN 978-1-59017-737-2

Printed in the United States of America on acid-free paper.
10 9 8 7 6 5 4 3 2 1

CONTENTS

AGOSTINO

I

IN THE early days of summer, Agostino and his mother used to go out to sea every morning on a small rowboat typical of Mediterranean beaches known as a *pattino*. At first she brought a boatman along with them, but Agostino gave such clear signs of annoyance at the man's presence that the oars were then turned over to him. He rowed with deep pleasure on the smooth, diaphanous, early-morning sea, and his mother, sitting in front of him, would speak to him softly, as joyful and serene as the sea and sky, as if he were a man rather than a thirteen-year-old boy. Agostino's mother was a big and beautiful woman still in her prime, and Agostino was filled with pride every time he got in the boat with her for one of their morning rides. All the bathers on the beach seemed to be watching, admiring his mother and envying him. Convinced that all eyes were on him, he felt as if he were speaking louder than usual, behaving in a special way, enveloped in a theatrical, exemplary air as if, rather than on a beach, his mother and he were onstage before an audience of hundreds of watchful eyes. Sometimes she would appear in a new bathing suit, and he could not help but make a loud remark, secretly hoping that others would overhear him. Or she would send him to fetch something from their cabin, while she stood waiting on the shore by the boat. He would obey with a hidden joy, happy to prolong the spectacle of their departure, if only for a few moments. Finally they would climb on board the boat, and Agostino would take hold of the oars and push off. But the intensity of his filial vanity and the turmoil of his infatuation would linger for many years to come.

When they were a good distance from the shore, the mother would tell her son to stop, and she would put on a rubber bathing cap, remove her sandals, and slip into the water. Agostino would follow. They would swim around the *pattino*, whose oars had been left unsecured, conversing in merry voices that echoed loudly over the silent sea, calm and filled with light. Sometimes the mother would point to a piece of cork floating in the distance and challenge her son to a race. She would give him a short lead and then, with powerful strokes, take off toward the cork. Or they would have diving competitions, breaching the clear smooth water with their bodies. Agostino would see the mother's body plunge into a circle of green bubbles, and he would jump in right after her, ready to follow her anywhere, even to the bottom of the sea. He would dive into the mother's wake and feel as if even the cold compact water conserved traces of the passage of that beloved body. After the swim, they would climb back on board, and the mother, looking around herself at the calm and luminous sea, would say, "Isn't it lovely today?" Agostino didn't reply because his pleasure in the beauty of the sea and sky was related, he felt, mainly to the profound intimacy of his relations with his mother. Without that intimacy, he sometimes found himself thinking, would it still be so beautiful? The two of them would dry themselves languorously in the sun, which became more ardent with the approach of midday. Then the mother would stretch out on the plank connecting the twin hulls of the boat. Lying on her back with her hair in the water, face to the sky, and eyes closed, she appeared to doze off. All the while Agostino, in his seat, would look around, look at the mother, and hold his breath lest he disturb her sleep. Occasionally she would open her eyes and say how good it felt to lie on her back with her eyes closed and feel the water rippling and flowing underneath her. Or she would ask Agostino to pass her the cigarette case, or better yet to light a cigarette and pass it to her, which Agostino would do with tremulous, painstaking care. Then the mother would smoke in silence, and Agostino would remain hunched over, his back to her but his head twisted to the side, so as to catch the little puffs of blue smoke that indicated where her head was resting, her hair radiating out in the water. Then the mother, who never seemed to tire of the sun, would ask Agostino to row and not turn around: in the meantime she would remove the top of her bathing suit and lower the bottoms so as to expose her whole body to the sunlight. Agostino rowed and felt proud of his assignment, as if it were a ritual in which he was allowed to participate. Not only did he never think of turning around but he felt as if her body, lying there behind him, naked in the sun, was shrouded in a mystery to which he owed the greatest veneration.

One morning the mother was under the beach umbrella, and Agostino, sitting on the sand next to her, was awaiting the hour when they usually went for their row. All at once a shadow obstructed the sunlight shining down on him: Looking up, he saw a tanned, dark-haired young man extending a hand to the mother. He paid him no mind, thinking it was the usual chance encounter, and moving away a bit, he waited for the conversation to end. But the young man did not accept an offer to sit down. Pointing toward the shore at the white *pattino* he'd arrived on, he invited the mother to accompany him on a boat ride out to sea. Agostino was sure she would turn down the invitation, like the many others that had preceded it. Much to his surprise, he saw her readily accept, gathering her things—sandals, bathing cap, and bag—and jumping to her feet. She had welcomed the young man's proposal with the same friendly and spontaneous ease that characterized her relations with her son. And with the same ease and spontaneity, she turned to Agostino, who had remained seated with his head bowed, intent on the sand sifting through his clenched fist, and told him to go ahead and have a swim by himself; she was going for a short ride and would be back in a little while. The young man, in the meantime, with a self-assured air, was already on his way to the boat. The woman was walking behind him, meekly, with her usual languid and majestic serenity. Looking at them, the son could not help but admit that the pride, vanity, and emotion he had felt during their outings on the sea must now be in the young man's heart. He saw the mother climb aboard the boat and the young man, his body leaning back and his feet planted firmly, pull the boat away from the shallow waters of the shore with a few vigorous strokes. The young man rowed, the mother sat in front of him, holding on to the seat with both hands, and they seemed to be chatting. Then the boat grew smaller and smaller, entered into the blinding light that the sun spread over the surface of the sea, and slowly dissolved into it.

Left alone, Agostino stretched out on his mother's lounge chair and, with one arm tucked behind his neck and his eyes fixed on the sky, adopted a pensive and indifferent attitude. Since every bather on the beach must have noticed his trips with his mother in the past few days, they would have remarked that today she had left him behind to go off with the young boatman. This was why he must not betray the annoyance and disappointment that he was feeling. But try as he might to feign an air of composure and serenity, he still felt that everyone could read in his face how forced and petty his attitude was. What offended him most wasn't so much the mother's preference for the young man as the quick almost premeditated joy with which she accepted his invitation. It was as if she had decided not to let the opportunity slip away and to seize it without hesitation as soon as it presented itself. It was as if all those days on the sea with him she had been bored and had only come along for lack of better company. One memory confirmed his ill humor. He had gone to a ball at a friend's house with his mother. During the first dance, a female cousin who was upset at being ignored by the men consented to dance a couple of rounds with him, the boy in short pants. But she had danced gracelessly, with a long sullen face. And although he was absorbed in minding his dance steps, Agostino quickly picked up on her unkind and contemptuous attitude. All the same he invited her for a third round and was surprised to see her smile and stand up quickly, smoothing out the wrinkles in her skirt with both hands. But rather than run into his arms, she walked past him toward a young man who, looming behind Agostino, had beckoned to her to dance. The scene lasted no longer than five seconds, and no one noticed except Agostino. But he was mortified beyond measure and had the impression that everyone had witnessed his humiliation.

Now, after his mother's departure with the young man

in the *pattino*, he compared the two events and found them identical. Like his cousin, his mother had been waiting for the right opportunity to abandon him. Like his cousin, and with the same breathless ease, she had accepted the first partner to come along. And in both cases, it had been his fate to fall from the summit of an illusion and crash to the ground, aching and bruised.

The mother stayed out on the water for a couple of hours that day. From under the beach umbrella he saw her step back onto the shore, hold out her hand to the young man, and with her head lowered under the noonday sun, make her leisurely way to the changing cabin. The beach was empty at that hour, a consolation for Agostino, who was still convinced that everyone was staring at them. "How did your morning go?" his mother asked indifferently. "I had a lot of fun," Agostino began, and he pretended that he, too, had gone out on the water with the boys from the next cabin. But she had already stopped listening and was running toward the cabin to get dressed. Agostino decided that the next day, as soon as he saw the young man's white *pattino* appear on the horizon, he would find some excuse to wander off and avoid having to suffer the insult of being left behind for a second time. But the next day, the minute he started to leave, he heard his mother calling him back. "Come," she said, standing up and gathering their things, "we're going for a boat ride." Agostino followed her, thinking that she intended to send the young man on his way and spend the morning alone with him. The young man was standing on the *pattino* waiting for them. The mother said hello and added simply, "I am bringing my son, too." And so a very unhappy Agostino found himself sitting next to the mother, facing the young man as he rowed.

Agostino had always seen the mother in one way: dignified, serene, and discreet. So he was bewildered, during the
ride, to see the change that had taken place not only in her
manner and speech but also apparently in her person, as if
she were no longer the same woman. They had barely entered
the open sea when the mother—in a sharp, allusive, and, to
Agostino, obscure remark—began a strange private conversation. As far as he could tell, it concerned a girlfriend of
the young man who had another more fortunate and acceptable suitor. But this was only a pretext and the conversation continued, insinuating, insistent, spiteful, malicious.
The mother seemed the more aggressive of the two yet also
the more defenseless. The young man took care to answer
her with a calm, almost ironic self-assurance. Sometimes
the mother seemed unhappy and even irritated with the
young man, to Agostino's delight. But a few seconds later,
she would disappoint him with a flirtatious remark that de-
stroyed this first impression. Or she would address the
young man in a resentful tone of voice with a series of obscure criticisms. But rather than take offense, the young
man, Agostino observed, wore an expression of fatuous vanity, and Agostino concluded that the reproach was only on
the surface, a cover for an affection he could not grasp. Both
the mother and the youth seemed to ignore his existence, as
if he wasn't there. She went so far with this display of ne-
glect as to remind the young man that going out with him
alone the day before had been a mistake on her part that
would never be repeated. From now on the son would always be present—an argument Agostino considered offen-
sive, as if rather than a person endowed with an independent
will he were an object that could be moved about arbitrarily.
Only once did the mother seem to notice his presence,

when the young man, suddenly letting go of the oars, leaned forward with an intensely malicious expression and whispered a short sentence to her that Agostino couldn't make out. This sentence had the power to make the mother jump up with exaggerated outrage and feigned horror. "At least show some consideration for this innocent boy," she answered, pointing to Agostino sitting by her side. Hearing himself called innocent, Agostino shook with repulsion, as if he had been struck by a dirty rag he couldn't dodge.

When they were a good distance from the shore, the young man proposed that the mother take a swim. Here Agostino, who had so often admired the discretion and ease with which she usually slipped into the water, could not help but be bewildered and pained by the new gestures with which she embellished her former behavior. The young man had plunged into the sea and already reemerged while the mother was still hesitantly testing the water with her toes, feigning either fear or reluctance—it was hard to tell. She covered herself, protested, laughing and holding on to the boat. Finally she lowered a leg and a hip into the water in an almost indecent pose, and let herself fall awkwardly into the arms of her companion. The two of them went under together, and together they floated back to the surface. Agostino, huddled in a corner, saw the smiling face of the mother next to the tanned and serious face of the youth, and it looked to him as if their cheeks were touching. In the clear water you could see the two bodies rubbing against each other, as if they wanted to intertwine, bumping their legs and their hips. Agostino glanced at them, then at the distant beach, and felt embarrassed and in the way. At the sight of his frowning face, the mother, treading water, uttered a sentence that humiliated and mortified him for the second time that morning: "Why the long face?... Can't you see how lovely the water is? Goodness, what a grumpy son I have." Agostino did not reply, limiting himself to casting his eyes elsewhere. The swim lasted for a long time. The mother and her companion played in the water like two dolphins and appeared to forget him entirely. Finally they climbed back on board. The youth leapt up in a single bound and then leaned over to pull up the mother, who was imploring his assistance from the water. Agostino watched. He observed how the youth's hands, in order to lift the woman, dug their fingers into her tanned skin where the arm is softest and widest, between the shoulder and the armpit. Then she sat down by Agostino, gasping for air, and with her pointed nails she pulled at her wet bathing suit so it wouldn't adhere too closely to the tips of her nipples and the roundness of her breasts. But Agostino remembered that when they were alone, the mother, a strong woman, had no need of any assistance in climbing back on the boat, and he attributed her begging for help and the wriggling of her body—apparently indulging in a feminine clumsiness—to the new spirit that had already caused so many and such unpleasant changes in her. He could not help but think that the mother, a large and dignified woman, was feeling her size as an impediment she would gladly be rid of, and her dignity, a boring habit that she now needed to replace with some awkward playfulness.

Once the two of them were back on the boat, the return trip began. This time the oars were assigned to Agostino, while the mother and the boatman sat on the plank between the hulls. He started rowing very slowly, in the scorching sun, sometimes wondering at the meaning of the voices, laughter, and movements behind his back. Every so often the mother, as if remembering he was there, would reach out an arm and give him an awkward pat on the back, or tickle him under the arms, asking him whether he was tired. "No, I'm not tired," Agostino would reply. When he heard the young man say, with a laugh, "It's good for him to row," he gave the oars a hard, angry tug. The mother leaned her head against Agostino's seat and kept her long legs outstretched, this much he could tell, but he had the impression this position was not always maintained. At one point, he heard a scrambling and what seemed to be a brief struggle. The mother sounded like she was choking. She stood up, stammering something, and the boat tipped to one side. For a moment the mother's belly rubbed against Agostino's cheek. It felt as vast as the sky and was beating strangely, as if it had a life that didn't belong to her or had slipped past her control. "I'll sit back down," she said, standing with her legs wide and her hands gripping her son's shoulders, "if you promise to behave." "I promise," came the young man's reply, with a false and playful solemnity. She lowered herself awkwardly onto the plank, brushing her belly against her son's cheek. A trace of moisture from the wet bathing suit was left on Agostino's skin and a deeper warmth seemed to evaporate the moisture into steam. Although he felt a sharp stab of murky repulsion, he obstinately refused to dry himself off.

As soon as they were close to shore, the young man leapt agilely onto the seat and, grabbing hold of the oars, pushed Agostino away, forcing him to sit next to the mother. She immediately put her arm around his waist, an unusual and, at the moment, unjustified gesture, asking him "How are you doing? Are you happy?" in a tone that did not seem to require an answer. She looked exceedingly happy and burst into song, another unusual occurrence, in a melodious voice with pathetic trills that made Agostino's skin crawl. While she was singing, she continued to hug him to her side, drenching him with the water seeping from her bathing suit, which her acrid, violent animal warmth seemed to heat and turn to sweat. And so, with the woman singing, the annoyed son surrendering to her embrace, and the young man rowing—a picture Agostino found contrived and false—they came ashore.

The next day, the young man reappeared. The mother brought Agostino along, and the same acts as the day before were repeated. Then, after a two-day interruption, there was another boat ride. Finally, having apparently achieved a certain intimacy with the mother, the young man began coming every morning to pick her up, and every morning Agostino was forced to accompany them and witness their conversations and frolicking in the water. These outings so repelled him that he sought any number of excuses to avoid them. Sometimes he would disappear and not come back until the mother, after calling him and looking for him for what seemed like hours, forced him to show his face not so much through her scolding as through the feelings of pity her annoyance and disappointment provoked in him. At other times he would start sulking on the boat, hoping the two of them would understand and leave him alone. But in the end he was always weaker and more sympathetic than his mother or the young man. For them, it was enough that he be there. His own feelings, he quickly came to see, were of little concern to them. So despite his best efforts, the outings continued.

One day Agostino was sitting on the sand behind the

mother's lounge chair, waiting for the white boat to appear on the horizon and the mother to wave a greeting and call to the young man by his name. But the usual hour of his appearance had come and gone, and the mother's disappointed and annoyed expression revealed that she had given up hoping for his arrival. Agostino had often wondered how he would feel in such an event, and he had always thought his joy would have been at least as great as his mother's dejection. He was surprised to discover, instead, that all he felt was empty disappointment, and he realized that the humiliation and repulsion of the daily outings had almost become his reason for living. So more than once, out of a murky, unconscious desire to make his mother suffer, he asked her whether they were going out to sea that day for their usual ride. And every time she gave the same answer: that she didn't know, but in all likelihood they would not be going today. She was sitting in her lounge chair, a book open on her knees, but she wasn't reading. With the gaze of a person searching for something in vain, her eyes often migrated to the sea, which meanwhile had filled with bathers and boats. After spending a long time behind her chair, Agostino crawled through the sand to face her and repeat in what even he knew was a nagging and almost sarcastic voice, "I can't believe it! We're not going out to sea today?" Maybe the mother detected the sarcasm and his desire to hurt her. Or maybe these rash words were enough to cause a pent-up irritation to erupt. She raised a hand and gave his cheek a sudden backhand slap, a blow that felt soft, almost accidental and regretful. Agostino didn't say a word. He did a somersault on the sand and walked off, making his way down the beach, head lowered, in the direction of the cabins. "Agostino ... Agostino," he heard her calling over and over again. Then the calls stopped, and turning around he thought he could discern, amid the many boats crowding the sea, the young man's white *pattino*. But by then he had stopped caring. With the same sharp sense of discovery as a man who has found a treasure and sneaks away to hide it and gaze upon it at his leisure, he ran to be alone with her slap, so new to him as to seem unbelievable.

His cheek was burning, and his eyes welled up with tears that he struggled to hold back. Fearing they would overflow before he had found a refuge, he ran hunched over. The bitterness that had been building during the long days when he was forced to accompany the young man and the mother was now being murkily disgorged. He felt as if, by unburdening himself with a good cry, he would finally understand something about these obscure events. When he reached the cabin, he hesitated for a moment, looking for a place to hide. He figured the easiest thing would be to take refuge inside. The mother would be out at sea, and no one would disturb him. Agostino raced up the steps, opened the door, and without closing it entirely went to sit on a stool in a corner.

He huddled with his knees to his chest and his head against the wall. Taking his face between his hands, he began to cry in earnest. Between his tears he could feel the sting of that slap. He wondered why such a harsh blow had felt so irresolute and soft. The burning sense of humiliation it provoked rekindled and even amplified a thousand unpleasant sensations that he had felt over the past few days. The one that returned to him most insistently was the memory of his mother's belly clothed in the wet fabric, pressed against his cheek, trembling and agitated by a lustful vitality. In the same way that beating old clothes raises big clouds of dust, that unjust blow, unleashed by the mother's impatience, reawakened in him the distinct sensation of her belly pressed against his cheek. At times that sensation seemed to replace the stinging left by the blow. At other times the two blended together, throbbing and burning as one. But while he understood the persistence of the slap, rekindling on his cheek every so often like a dying fire, the reasons for the tenacious survival of that distant sensation remained obscure. Of the many, why had this one remained so indelible and so vivid? He had no answer. But he felt that as long as he lived, he would only need to recall the moment to feel against his cheek once more the throbbing of her belly and the moist coarseness of her wet bathing suit.

He cried softly so as not to disturb the painful workings of memory. As the tears slowly but steadily trickled from his eyes, he rubbed them with his fingertips against his moist skin. A sparse and sultry darkness filled the cabin. He suddenly had the feeling the door was opening, and he almost hoped his mother, repentant and affectionate, would place one hand on his shoulder and, with the other, take him by the chin and turn him around to face her. He was already preparing his lips to whisper "Mamma," when he heard footsteps enter the cabin and the door close behind them, but no hand came to rest on his shoulders or pat him on the head.

Then he looked up and stared. He saw a boy who appeared to be about his age standing by the door, in the attitude of a lookout. He was wearing shorts with rolled-up cuffs and a worn-out sleeveless T-shirt with a big hole in the back. A thin blade of sunlight shone through the cracks between the boards of the cabin and burnished a head of tight copper-colored curls above the nape of the neck. Barefoot, his hands on the doorjamb, the boy scoured the beach and didn't seem aware of Agostino's presence.

Agostino dried his eyes with the back of his hand and started to say, "Hey you, over there. What are you looking for?" But the other boy turned and gestured to him to keep quiet. Turning around he revealed an ugly freckled face whose most remarkable feature was his glowering blue eyes. Agostino thought he recognized him. He was a son of a lifeguard or boatman. He must have seen the boy pushing off the boats or doing something like that near the beach, he thought.

"We're playing cops and robbers," the boy said a few seconds later, facing Agostino. "I don't want them to see me."

"Which one are you?" asked Agostino, quickly drying his tears.

"A robber, of course," the boy replied without looking at him.

Agostino took a good look at the boy. He didn't know whether he liked him, but he spoke in a rough dialect that was new to Agostino and sparked his curiosity. Besides which, he sensed instinctively that the boy hiding in the cabin represented an opportunity—what kind of opportunity he couldn't say—and he shouldn't let it slip away.

"Can I play, too?" he asked boldly.

The other boy turned and gave him an insolent look. "Who do you think you are?" he said quickly. "We only let our friends play."

"So," Agostino said with a shameful insistence, "let me play, too."

The boy shrugged his shoulders saying, "It's too late now, the game's almost over."

"So let me play the next time."

"There isn't going to be a next time," the boy said, skeptical and almost amazed at such insistence. "After this we're going to the pine grove."

"If you'll take me I can come, too."

The boy started laughing, both amused and contemptuous. "Get a load of you. Forget about it, we don't want you."

Agostino had never found himself in such a situation, but the same instinct that prompted him to ask the boy if he could play was now making him beg for acceptance. "Listen," he said hesitatingly, "if... if you let me join your group, I'll give you something."

The other boy turned around immediately, his eyes alive with greed.

"Whatcha got?"

"Anything you want."

"Tell me everything you're gonna give me."

Agostino pointed to a big toy sailboat, with all its sails still attached, lying at the other end of the cabin surrounded by odds and ends.

"I'll give you that boat."

"What am I supposed to do with it?" said the boy, shrugging his shoulders.

"You can sell it," Agostino proposed.

"They won't take it from me," the boy said with an experienced air. "They'd say it was stolen."

Despairing, Agostino took a look around. His mother's clothes were hanging from a wall hook. Her shoes were on the floor, and on a side table a kerchief and a few other objects. There seemed to be nothing in the cabin he could offer.

"Hey," said the boy, noticing his bewilderment. "You got any cigarettes?"

Agostino remembered how that morning his mother had put two packs of very fine cigarettes in the large bag hanging from a wall hook. Triumphant, he was quick to answer. "Of course, yes, cigarettes I do have. Do you want them?"

"You have to ask?" said the boy with an ironic sneer. "You're such a dope. Give 'em here, quick."

Agostino unhooked the bag from the coatrack, rummaged around inside it, and pulled out the two packs. He showed them to the boy as if he couldn't tell how many cigarettes he wanted.

"Gimme both," the boy said offhandedly, snatching both packs from him. He checked the brand name, clucked his tongue in appreciation, and added, "Say, you must be rich."

Agostino didn't know what to answer. The boy continued. "I'm Berto. Who are you?"

Agostino said his name, but the boy had already stopped listening. Breaking the paper seal and opening one of the packs with impatient fingers, he took out a cigarette and brought it to his lips. Then he took a kitchen match from his pocket, scratched it against the cabin wall to light it, and, after a first puff of smoke, took another cautious peek out the door.

"Come on, we're going," he said after a moment, gesturing to Agostino to follow him. One after the other, they stepped out of the cabin.

On the beach, Berto immediately headed for the road behind the row of cabins.

Walking across the scorching sand, through a thicket of juniper and thistle bushes, he said, "Now we're going to the den. The other guys have left by now and are looking for me up that way."

"Where's the den?" Agostino asked.

"By the Vespucci beach stand." He held the cigarette vainly, as if to flaunt it, and with a rugged sensuality took a long drag. "You don't smoke?" he asked Agostino.

"I don't much care for it," Agostino answered. He was too ashamed to admit that the idea had never occurred to him.

But Berto laughed. "Fess up, you don't smoke because your mom won't let you." He said these words in an unkind, even disdainful manner. He held out the cigarette to Agostino and said, "Come on, give it a try."

They had reached the promenade and were walking barefoot on the sharp gravel between the dried-up flower beds. Agostino brought the cigarette to his lips and took a tiny puff, immediately coughing it out.

Berto laughed scornfully. "You call that smoking?" he exclaimed. "That's not how you do it. Here, let me show you." He took the cigarette and inhaled deeply, rolling his surly, listless blue eyes, then he opened his mouth wide and brought it close to Agostino's face. His mouth was empty, with the tongue curling at the back of his palate.

"Get a good look," Berto said, closing his mouth. He blew a cloud of smoke right into Agostino's face. Agostino coughed and giggled in panic. "Now you try," Berto added.

A streetcar passed by, whistling, shaking its curtains in the wind. Agostino took another big puff and with a painful effort inhaled the smoke. But it went down the wrong way and he started coughing quite pathetically. Berto took the cigarette and giving him a pat on the back said, "Good boy... I can see you're a big smoker."

After this experiment they walked along in silence. One bathing establishment followed the other, with their rows of cabins painted in pastel colors, tilted beach umbrellas, and idiotic triumphal arches. In between the cabins you could see the crowded beach and hear the festive buzzing. The sparkling sea was filled with bathers.

"Where is Vespucci beach?" Agostino asked, quickening his pace to keep up with his new friend.

"It's the last one."

Agostino wondered whether he shouldn't turn back: If his mother hadn't gone out on the boat, she would surely be looking for him. But the memory of that slap stifled this last scruple. He felt as if, by going off with Berto, he were pursuing an obscure and justified form of revenge. "What about smoke in your nose?" Berto suddenly asked him. "Do you know how to exhale through your nostrils?"

Agostino shook his head. With the cigarette butt stuck between his lips, Berto inhaled the smoke and blew it out through his nostrils. "Watch me," he added, "I'm going to make the smoke come out of my eyes. Now put your hand on my chest and look me in the eyes." Unsuspecting, Agostino approached him, placed his palm over the boy's chest, and stared at his pupils, waiting to see if smoke really would come out. But the boy tricked him by suddenly stubbing out the lit cigarette on the back of Agostino's hand and jumped for joy as he tossed away the butt, shouting, "You fell for it. What a dope...what a dope!"

The pain was blinding, and Agostino's first impulse was to throw himself at Berto and start punching him. But the other boy, seeing him run toward him, stood still, placed his fists against Agostino's chest, and with two hard blows to his stomach, almost knocked him out and left him gasping for air. "You want to make something of it?" he said maliciously. "There's more where that came from." Furious, Agostino charged him again, but he felt weak and destined to lose. This time Berto grabbed him, stuck his head under his arm, and started to choke Agostino, who had stopped struggling and was begging Berto in a strangled voice to let him go. Berto released him and, with a backward jump, landed on both feet in combat position. But Agostino had heard the vertebrae of his neck crackle. He was not so much frightened as bewildered by the boy's extraordinary brutality. It seemed incredible that he, Agostino, whom everyone had always liked, could now be hurt so deliberately and ruthlessly. Most of all he was bewildered and troubled by this ruthlessness, a new behavior so monstrous it was almost attractive.

"What did I ever do to you?" he said, gasping for air. "I gave you the cigarettes... and you..." His eyes welled up with tears before he could finish the sentence.

"Crybaby," Berto barked sarcastically. "You want your cigarettes back? I don't need your cigarettes. Take 'em and go back to your mamma."

"It doesn't matter," Agostino said disconsolately, shaking his head. "I was just talking... you can keep them."

"Let's forget about it," Berto said. "We're here."

Agostino, bringing his burned hand to his mouth, looked up and stared. On this stretch of the shore there was only a handful of cabins, five or six at most, situated far apart from each other. They were shabby, built from rough wood, and between them you could see the beach and sea, both equally deserted. A small group of working-class women were in the shade of a boat pulled ashore, some standing, others lying on the sand, all of them wearing outmoded black bathing suits with long white-trimmed trunks, busy drying themselves and exposing their milky-white limbs to the sun. An arch with a blue sign carried the words, BAGNO AMERIGO VESPUCCI. A low green shack sunken in the sand indicated the lifeguard's place. Past the Vespucci beach, the coast extended as far as the eye could see, devoid of cabins on the beach or houses along the road, an isolated patch of windbeaten sand between the sparkling blue sea and the dusty green pine grove.

From the road, one side of the shack was concealed by the dunes, which were higher here than elsewhere along the shore. Once the two boys had reached the top of the dunes, they came across a faded, rust-red tarp full of patches and apparently cut from the sail of an old fishing trawler. Two corners of the tarp were tied to poles stuck in the sand while the other two were attached to the shack.

"That's the den," Berto said.

Under the tarp a man was sitting at a wobbly table, lighting a cigar. He was surrounded by two or three boys stretched out on the sand. Berto broke into a run and dropped to the man's feet, shouting, "Den!" Feeling somewhat embarrassed, Agostino approached the group. "And this is Pisa," Berto said, pointing to Agostino, who was amazed at the nickname given to him so quickly. It had only been five minutes since he told Berto he was born in Pisa.

Agostino lay down on the ground, too. The sand under the tarp was not as clean as on the beach. Watermelon rinds, wood splinters, green pottery shards, and all kinds of debris were strewn together. In places the sand was hard and crusty from buckets of dirty water tossed out of the shack.

Agostino noticed that the boys, four in all, were dressed in clothes that were ragged and torn. Like Berto, they must have been the children of boatmen and lifeguards. "He was at Speranza beach," Berto said in one breath, still speaking about Agostino. "He says he wants to play cops and robbers with us...but the game is over, isn't it? I told you the game was over."

Suddenly there were shouts of "It doesn't count! It doesn't count!" Agostino looked and saw running toward them from the sea a group of boys, probably the cops. The first was a boy of about sixteen, short and stocky, in a bathing suit. Then, to Agostino's great surprise, came a black boy. The third was a blond, and from his bearing and the beauty of his body, Agostino thought he must be of more noble origin than the others. But when he drew near, his torn and threadbare bathing suit and a certain simplicity in his handsome face with its big blue eyes showed plainly that he, too, was poor. The first three boys were followed by four more, all about the same age, between thirteen and fourteen. The stocky one was by far the oldest, and at first impression it was surprising that he would be hanging around with such a young crowd. But his pasty face with its dull, inexpressive features provided, in its brutal stupidity, the reason for this unusual association. He had almost no neck, and his smooth, hairless torso was as wide at the waist and hips as it was at the shoulders. "You hid in a cabin," he shouted violently at Berto. "Try to deny it. The rules said no cabins."

"I did not," Berto replied just as violently. "Tell him, Pisa," he added, turning to Agostino. "It's not true that I hid in a cabin. Me and him were behind the corner of the Speranza stand. We saw you going by, didn't we, Pisa?"

"Actually," said Agostino, who was incapable of lying, "you were hiding in my cabin."

"See, I knew it!" the older boy shouted, shaking his fist under Berto's nose. "I'll smash your head in, you big liar."

"Squealer," Berto shouted in Agostino's face. "I told you to stay where you were. Go back to your mamma." He was filled with an uncontainable, animal violence that amazed Agostino in some obscure way. But while he was shouting, one of the cigarette packs fell out of his pocket. He went to pick it up, but the older boy was quicker. Diving to the ground, he grabbed it and shook it in the air triumphantly. "Cigarettes, eh," he shouted, "cigarettes."

"Give 'em back," Berto shouted, throwing himself at him furiously. "They're mine, Pisa gave them to me, give 'em back or I'll—"

The other boy took a step back and waited till Berto was within range. Then he stuck the cigarette pack between his teeth and started methodically pounding Berto's stomach with his fists. Then, tripping him, he sent him sprawling to the ground. "Give 'em back," Berto shouted again as he squirmed in the sand. But the other boy shouted with a dumb laugh, "He's got more. Get busy, guys ..." and with a unity that shocked Agostino, the boys piled on top of Berto. For a moment there was a tangle of bodies in a cloud of sand at the feet of the man, who continued to smoke while leaning against the table. Finally the blond, who appeared to be the most agile, disentangled himself from the pile, stood up, and waved the second cigarette pack in the air triumphantly. One by one the rest of them stood up. Berto was last. His ugly freckled face was twisted with rage. "You dogs ... you thieves," he shouted, shaking his fist and sobbing. He was crying angry tears, and it had a strange effect on Agostino to see the tables turned on his tormentor and Berto treated just as ruthlessly as Berto had treated him. "You dogs ... you dogs," Berto cried again. The older boy approached and delivered a hard slap to Berto's face, which made the other boys jump for joy. "Are you ready to cut it out?" Enraged, Berto ran to the corner of the shack and stooped down to grab with both hands a huge rock that he threw at his enemy. The other boy dodged it easily with a derisive whistle. "Pigs!" Berto cried, sobbing, but keeping a cautious distance from behind the corner of the shack. His body was wracked with sobs. The fury was even in his tears, which seemed to release a pent-up bitterness, vulgar and repellant. But his companions had already forgotten him and lain back down on the sand. The older boy opened one pack of cigarettes and the blond opened the other. All of a sudden the man sitting at the table, who had observed the fight without making a move, said, "Hand 'em over."

Agostino looked at the man. He was big and fat, probably a few years shy of fifty. He had a sly and coldly benevolent face. Bald, with an odd saddle-shaped forehead, small squinting eyes, a red aquiline nose, and flared nostrils covered with purple veins that were disgusting to see. He had a drooping mustache over a slightly crooked mouth that was chomping on a cigar. He was wearing a faded overshirt and a pair of turquoise cotton trousers, one leg down to his ankle, and the other rolled up to his knee. A black sash was wrapped around his belly. A final detail added to Agostino's initial disgust. He realized that Saro, as the lifeguard was called, did not have five fingers on each enormous hand but rather six, making them look more like stumpy tentacles than fingers. Agostino studied his hands at length but could not tell whether Saro had two index fingers, two middle fingers, or two ring fingers. They all seemed to be the same length, except the little finger, which protruded from his hand like a thin branch at the base of a knotty tree trunk. Saro took the cigar butt from his mouth and repeated simply, "The cigarettes."

The blond stood up and went to set the pack on the table. "Good boy, Sandro," said Saro.

"What if I don't want to?" the older boy shouted defiantly.

"Come on, Tortima. You'd better hand them over," shouted voices from all sides. Tortima looked around and then at Saro who, with the six fingers of his right hand wrapped around the cigarette pack, was staring at him through narrowed eyes. Sighing, "All right, but it's not fair," Tortima stood up and put the other pack on the table as well.

"Now I'll divvy them up," said Saro in a soft and friendly voice. Without removing the cigar from his mouth, squinting his eyes, he opened one of the packs, took out a cigarette with stubby multiple fingers that seemed unable to clench it, and tossed it to the black boy, "Here, Homs." He took another cigarette and tossed it to another boy. A third flew into the cupped hands of Sandro. A fourth hit Tortima straight in his stolid face. And so it went. "Want one?" he asked Berto, who having swallowed his tears had come back, as quiet as a mouse, to lie down among his buddies. Chastened, he nodded yes, and a cigarette was launched in his direction. Once each of the boys had received a cigarette, he started to close the still half-full pack, but he stopped and asked Agostino, "Hey you, Pisa. Want one?" Agostino would have said no, but Berto gave him a punch in the ribs whispering, "Ask for it, you dummy. Then we can smoke it together." Agostino said yes and got his cigarette too. Then Saro closed the pack.

"What about the other ones . . . the other ones?" the boys all shouted.

"The other ones you'll get in the next few days," Saro answered calmly. "Pisa, take these cigarettes and put them back in the shack."

No one breathed a word. Agostino clumsily took the two packs and, stepping over the reclining boys, made his way to the shack and entered. There appeared to be only one room, and he liked its smallness, like a house in a fairy tale. The ceiling was low, with white beams and unpainted walls of rough planks. A dim subdued light entered the room through two tiny windows, complete with windowsills, small square windowpanes, shutters, curtains, and even a few flowerpots. One corner was occupied by the bed, neatly made, with a bleached white pillow and a red blanket. In another corner there was a round table and three chairs. On the marble top of a chest of drawers were two bottles containing miniature sailboats or steamships. The walls were covered with sails hung from nails, oars, and other boating equipment. Agostino thought anyone who owned a shack like this, so small and cozy, must be truly enviable. He approached the table, on which there was a large chipped porcelain bowl filled with cigar butts, set down the two cigarette packs, and then came back out into the sunlight.

All of the boys, lying prone on the sand near Saro, were smoking with big demonstrative gestures of delight. They were talking about something he couldn't quite grasp. "I tell you it was him," Sandro was saying.

"His mother is pretty," an admiring voice said, "the best-looking woman on the beach. Homs and me, we snuck under her cabin to see her getting undressed, but she lowered her dress right on top of where we were looking and you couldn't see a thing...she's got nice legs...and those tits..."

"Her husband's never around," a third voice remarked.

"Don't worry. She knows how to console herself. You know who she's doing it with? That guy from Villa Sorriso...the dark-haired one. He comes to pick her up every day with his boat."

"You think he's the only one? She does it with anyone that asks," another boy said maliciously.

"Maybe, but I still say it's someone else," another one insisted.

"Hey, Pisa," Sandro asked Agostino authoritatively, "isn't your mother the lady at the Speranza beach? Tall, dark-haired, wears a two-piece striped bathing suit? With a beauty mark on the left, near her mouth?"

"Yes, why?" Agostino answered uneasily.

"It's him! I knew it was him!" Berto said triumphantly. And in a fit of malicious envy, "You're the third wheel, eh? Out on the boat it's you, her, and lover boy. That makes you the third wheel." His words were followed by gales of laughter. Even Saro was smiling beneath his mustache.

"I don't know what you're talking about," Agostino replied, blushing, uncomfortable and uncomprehending. He felt as if he should object, but these uncouth jokes aroused in him an unexpected, almost cruel feeling of pleasure, as if the boys had unknowingly avenged through their words all the humiliations that his mother had inflicted on him lately. At the same time he was horrified at how much they knew about his affairs.

"Don't play stupid with us," said the usual malicious voice.

"Who knows what they do. They always go so far out to sea. Tell me," Tortima grilled him with mock seriousness, "tell us what they do. He kisses her, right?" He placed the back of his hand against his lips and planted a big kiss on it.

"Actually," said Agostino, his face red with shame, "we go out to sea to go swimming."

"Oh, to go swimming," several voices said sarcastically.

"My mother goes swimming and so does Renzo."

"Ah, so his name is Renzo," one of the boys said confidently, as if he had discovered a lost thread in his memory. "Renzo . . . he's tall, tanned, right?"

"What do Renzo and your mamma do?" Berto suddenly asked, emboldened. "They"—and he made an expressive gesture with his hands—"and you sit there watching them, right?"

"Me?" Agostino repeated fearfully, looking all around. Everyone roared, smothering their laughter in the sand. Saro was the only one to observe him attentively, without moving a muscle or saying a word. Agostino gave him a look of despair, as if imploring him for help.

Saro seemed to understand his look. He took the cigar from his mouth and said, "Can't you see he knows nothing?"

A sudden silence followed the clamor. "How can he know nothing?" asked Tortima, who hadn't realized it.

"He knows nothing," Saro replied plainly. Then he turned to Agostino, lowering his voice. "Say, Pisa . . . a man and a woman . . . what do they do together? Do you know?"

Everyone seemed to be holding their breath. Agostino looked at Saro, who was smoking and studying him through half-closed eyes. He looked at the boys, who all seemed about to burst into laughter, then he repeated mechanically, as his eyes clouded over, "A man and a woman?"

"Yes, your mother and Renzo," Berto explained brutally.

Agostino wanted to say, "Don't talk about my mother." But he was so confused by the swarm of sensations and dark memories aroused in him by the question that he was left speechless.

"He doesn't know," Saro interrupted, switching his cigar from the right to the left corner of his mouth. "Come on, who wants to tell him?" Agostino looked around, dismayed. It was like being at school, but with what teacher and what pupils? "Me, me, me," all the boys shouted at once. For a moment Saro's uncertain gaze scanned all those faces inflamed in emulation. He said, "You guys don't really know either. You've only heard about it. Let someone who really knows about it do the talking." Agostino saw the boys go silent and look at one another. "Tortima," someone said. The boy's face lit up in a vain expression. He started to stand, but a rancorous Berto called out, "He made the whole thing up. It's a pack of lies." "What do you mean it's a pack of lies?" shouted Tortima, pouncing on Berto. "You're the liar, you little bastard." But this time Berto was too quick for him. He fled, poking his head out from behind a corner of the shack, making faces and sticking out his tongue at Tortima, who shook his fist at him threateningly and shouted, "Don't you dare come back." But Tortima's candidacy had been somewhat diminished by Berto's outburst. "Let Sandro tell him," all the boys cried in unison.

Handsome and elegant, his arms folded over a broad dark chest on which scattered blond hairs glittered like gold, Sandro stepped forward into the circle of boys reclining in the sand. Agostino noticed his strong tanned legs, which seemed enveloped in a cloud of gold dust. More blond hairs escaped from his groin, poking through the holes in his red swimming trunks. "It's very simple," he said in a strong clear voice. And speaking slowly and illustrating his points with gestures that were effective but not what might be considered vulgar, he explained to Agostino something he seemed to have always known and, as if in a deep sleep, forgotten. His explanation was followed by other less sober descriptions. Some of the boys made coarse hand gestures. Others repeated in loud voices words that were new and abhorrent to Agostino's ears. Two of them said, "Let's show him how to do it," and fell to the burning sand in each other's arms, shuddering and rubbing against each other. Sandro, pleased with his success, had withdrawn to the side and was finishing his cigarette in silence. "Now do you understand?" asked Saro, as soon as the hubbub had died down.

Agostino nodded. In reality he hadn't so much understood as absorbed the notion, the way you absorb a medicine or a poison and don't feel the effect immediately but know that the pain or the benefit will not be kept waiting much longer. The notion wasn't in his vacant, aching, befuddled mind but in another part of himself, in his heart swelling with bitterness, deep inside his chest, which was surprised to welcome it. It was not unlike a bright shiny object whose splendor makes it hard to look at directly and whose shape can thus barely be detected. It was as if he had always known but never felt it in his bones the way he did now.

"Renzo and Pisa's mother," he heard someone saying behind him. "I'll be Renzo and you be the mother. OK?" He pivoted around to see Berto who, with a coarse gesture and even more coarse formality, was bowing and asking another boy, "My lady, would it please you to go for a boat ride . . . to

go for a little dip in the sea...Pisa will accompany us."
Blinded by a burst of rage, he pounced on Berto, shouting,
"Don't talk about my mother!" But even before he knew
what had happened, he was flat on the ground, held in place
by Berto's knee while fists showered down on his face. He
wanted to cry, but knowing that tears would only lead to
more teasing, he made a supreme effort to restrain them.
He covered his face with one arm and lay there motionless,
as if he were dead. After a little while Berto let him go, and
Agostino, battered and bruised, went to sit at Saro's feet.
The voluble boys had already moved on to another topic.
One of them asked Agostino, point-blank, "Are you rich?"

By now Agostino was so intimidated he didn't know
what to say, but he answered anyway. "I think so."

"How much? One million? Two million? Three million?"

"I don't know," said Agostino, at a loss for words.

"Do you have a big house?"

"Yes," said Agostino. Reassured by the more polite tone
the dialogue was assuming, he couldn't resist boasting,
"We have twenty rooms."

"Twenty rooms," an admiring voice repeated.

"Wow," said another voice, incredulously.

"We have two living rooms," said Agostino, "and then
there's my father's study—"

"Get a load of him," one voice said.

"I mean, it used to be my father's," Agostino hastened to
add, almost hoping that this detail would attract the boys'
sympathy. "My father passed away."

There was a moment of silence. "So your mother's a
widow?" Tortima asked.

"Well, yeah," a few voices said jokingly.

"What difference does it make? She might have remarried," was Tortima's defense.

"No . . . she didn't remarry," said Agostino.

"Do you have a car, too?" another voice asked.

"Yes."

"And a driver?"

"Yes."

"Tell your mother I'm ready to be her driver," one boy shouted.

"What do you do with all those rooms?" asked Tortima, who seemed more impressed by Agostino's stories than anyone else. "Do you have balls?"

"Yes, my mother holds receptions," Agostino replied.

"There must be a lot of beautiful ladies," said Tortima, as if talking to himself. "How many people come?"

"I don't know."

"How many?"

"Twenty or thirty," replied Agostino, who was now feeling reassured and a little bit cocky about this success.

"Twenty or thirty . . . and what do they do?"

"What do you think they do," said Berto ironically. "They probably dance, have fun. They're rich, not poor slobs like us. They probably make love—"

"No, they don't make love," said Agostino earnestly, also to show that at this point he knew perfectly what the expression meant.

Tortima seemed to be struggling with an obscure idea he couldn't quite formulate. He finally said, "But if out of the blue, I were to show up at one of those receptions and say, 'Here I am,' what would you do?"

As he said this he got to his feet and went through the motions of someone introducing himself with a swagger, chest swelling, hands on his hips. The boys all burst out laughing.

"I would ask you to leave," said Agostino plainly, encouraged by the boys' laughter.

"And if I refused to leave?"

"I would have the waiters show you the door."

"You have waiters?" someone asked.

"No, but when we have receptions my mother hires them."

"Huh, just like your father." One of the boys must have been a waiter's son.

"And if I were to resist the waiters, punch them in the face and make my way to the middle of the room and shout, 'You're a bunch of crooks and bitches,' what would you say then?" Tortima insisted menacingly, walking up to Agostino and poking his fist under his nose, as if to make him smell it. But now everyone turned against Tortima, not to take Agostino's side so much as to hear more details about his fabulous wealth.

"Leave him alone. They'd kick you out and they'd be right," were the protests all around. With disdain Berto said, "Keep out of it. Your father's a sailor, and you're going to end up a sailor, too. And if you show up at Pisa's house you wouldn't be shouting a thing. I can almost see you," he added, jumping to his feet and mimicking Tortima's imagined deference at Agostino's house: "'Begging your pardon, is this the home of Master Pisa? Begging your pardon . . . I've come . . . it doesn't matter, my apologies . . . my apologies for the disturbance, I'll come back later.' I can almost see you. You'd be bowing all the way down the stairs."

All the boys laughed. Tortima, as stupid as he was brutal, didn't dare attack them for laughing, but still itching for retaliation he asked Agostino, "Do you know how to arm wrestle?"

"Arm wrestle?" Agostino repeated.

"He doesn't know what arm wrestling is," several derisive voices called out. Sandro took Agostino's arm, and bent it back, forcing his hand in the air and his elbow into the sand. Meanwhile Tortima had reclined on the sand, belly-down, and positioned his arm in the same manner. "You have to push in one direction," Sandro said, "while Tortima pushes in the other."

Agostino took Tortima's hand. With a single shove, Tortima had his arm flat on the ground and stood up triumphantly.

"My turn," said Berto, and with the same ease as Tortima he nailed Agostino's arm to the ground. "Me, me," shouted his pals. One after the other they each had a try and each one of them beat Agostino. The last to come forward was the black boy, and a voice said, "If you let Homs beat you, well, then your arms must be made out of rubber." Agostino decided that at least the black boy wouldn't beat him.

Homs had skinny arms the color of roast coffee. Agostino thought his own looked stronger. "Let's do it, Pisa," the boy said, boasting stupidly, laying down in front of him. He had a listless, almost feminine voice, and as soon as his face was only a foot away, Agostino could see that his nose wasn't flat, as he had imagined, but aquiline, small and turning in on itself like an oily black urchin, with a kind of clear, yellowish mole on one of his nostrils. His lips weren't as big as other black people's, but thin and purple. His eyes were round and white, oppressed by a swollen forehead from which a sooty mop of hair rose. "Let's do it, Pisa. I won't hurt you," he added, slipping into Agostino's palm a delicate hand with thin black fingers and pink fingernails. Agostino realized that if he pulled his upper arm a little closer, without appearing to do anything, he could put his whole weight behind his hand. At first this simple realization allowed him to resist and check Homs's exertions. For a long while they were in a standoff, surrounded by the attentive boys. Agostino's face was tense but firm. His whole body was straining while the black boy was grimacing, gritting his white teeth and squinting. "Pisa's winning," a voice said suddenly, amazed. But at that moment a terrible pain shot through Agostino from his shoulder and down his entire arm. Exhausted, he loosened his grip saying, "No, he's stronger than me." "The next time you'll beat me," said the black boy as he stood up, with his unpleasant, smarmy courtesy. "Even Homs beat you. You're really worthless," said Tortima scornfully. But now the boys seemed to have grown tired of teasing Agostino. "Let's jump in the water," one of them proposed. "Yes, yes, to the water," they all shouted. Skipping and tumbling, they ran across the beach, over the burning sand, toward the sea. Watching them from a distance, Agostino saw them jumping into the shallow water one after the other, headfirst like fish, with big splashes and shouts of joy. When he reached the shore, Tortima emerged from the water like an animal, first with his back and then with his head, shouting, "Jump in, Pisa. What are you doing over there?"

"I have my clothes on," Agostino said.

"Now I'm going to tear them off of you," replied Tortima mischievously. Agostino tried to run away but wasn't fast enough. Tortima grabbed hold of him, dragged him despite his efforts, and pulling him into the sea, held his head underwater, almost drowning him. Then he shouted, "See you later, Pisa," and swam off at a sprint. Not much farther away he saw Sandro standing on a *pattino*, maneuvering elegantly between the boys who clamored around him, trying to climb into the boat. Soaking wet and breathing heavily, Agostino returned to shore and for a moment looked back at the *pattino* crammed with boys on their way out to the deserted sea under a blinding sun. Then, walking quickly over the glassy sand lining the shore, he headed back to Speranza beach.

2

IT WASN'T as late as he had feared. Once he'd reached the beach, he found that his mother wasn't back yet. The beach was emptying. A few scattered swimmers still lingered in the dazzling sea. Everyone else, languid and overheated, was lined up beneath the midday sky, leaving by the boardwalk that led to the street. Agostino sat under the beach umbrella and waited. His mother's ride seemed to be lasting longer than usual. Forgetting that the young man had arrived late and that it hadn't been his mother who wanted to go alone but he who had disappeared, he told himself that the mother and the young man must have taken advantage of his absence to do the very things that Saro and the boys had talked about. The thought did not make him jealous; instead, it sent a shudder through him that was new and filled with complicity, curiosity, and smug, glum approval. It was right that his mother should behave in such a way with the young man, that she should go with him on the boat every day, and that at this very moment, far from prying eyes, between the sea and the sky, she should lose herself in his arms. It was right, and now he was perfectly capable of understanding it. While mulling over these thoughts, he scanned the horizon for the two lovers.

Finally the *pattino* appeared, no more than a white speck on the deserted sea, approaching rapidly. He saw his mother

sitting and the young man rowing. The oars lifted and lowered, and every stroke was accompanied by a splash of glit-
tering water. Agostino stood up and went to the water. He
wanted to see his mother getting off the boat, to observe
carefully any traces of the intimacy in which he had participated unknowingly for so long, and which now, after
the revelations of Saro and the boys, he thought would appear to him in a completely new light filled with indecent
telltale clues. From the *pattino*, even before it came to shore,
his mother gave him a big wave. Then she jumped into the
water cheerfully and in a few strides was by her son. "Are
you hungry? We're going to go have something to eat right
away. Goodbye, goodbye, see you tomorrow," she added in
a melodious voice, turning around and waving to the young
man. To Agostino she seemed happier than usual, and as he
followed behind her on the beach, he couldn't help but
think that her goodbyes to the young man conveyed an
elated pathetic joy, as if something the son's presence had
impeded so far had really happened that day. But his obser-
vations and suspicions stopped there. Besides, except for
that ungainly joyousness so unlike her customary dignity,
he couldn't understand what exactly had happened during
the ride and whether they had engaged in amorous relations. Face, neck, hands, body: no matter how closely he
studied them with his cruel new awareness, they showed no
sign of the kisses and caresses they had received. The more
Agostino looked at his mother, the more disgruntled he felt.

"The two of you were alone today, without me," he tried
to say while they headed toward the cabin, almost hoping
she would answer, "Yes, and we were finally able to make
love." But his mother seemed to interpret his words as an
allusion to the slap and his subsequent running away. "Let's

not speak about what happened anymore," she said, stopping for a moment, squeezing him by the shoulders and staring him in the face with her smiling excited eyes. "Agreed? I know that you love me. Give me a kiss, and not another word about it." Agostino suddenly found himself with his face against her neck, once so sweet with the perfume and warmth that enveloped her chastely. But beneath her lips he seemed to sense a new yet faint throbbing, like the last surge of the bitter lingering feeling the young man's mouth must have awakened in her flesh. The mother quickly climbed the stairs to the cabin. With his face blushing from a shame he could not understand, he lay down in the sand.

Later, on their way home, he ruminated at length, in the depths of his troubled heart, on these new and still-obscure sentiments. How strange it was that earlier, when he was still unaware of good and evil, his mother's mysterious relations with the young man had seemed ridden with guilt. Now that the revelations of Saro and his young acolytes had opened his eyes and confirmed those first painful suspicions of sensuality, he was filled with doubt and unsatisfied curiosity. Earlier, his spirit had been aroused by filial affection, jealous and naïve; now, in this cruel new light, his still undiminished affection had been replaced in part by an acrid disenchanted curiosity that found those first minor stirrings inconsequential. Earlier, every seemingly discordant word or gesture had offended him without enlightening him, and he had almost preferred to ignore them. Now that his eyes were always on her, the gaffes and missteps that used to upset him seemed insignificant, and he almost hoped to surprise her in one of the naked, shameless, natural poses he had just learned about from Saro and the boys.

The truth is, he might not have been seized by a desire to

spy on his mother and to destroy the aura of dignity and respect with which he had viewed her if, on that same day, chance had not set him so violently on this path. At home, mother and son ate almost without speaking. The mother appeared distracted, and Agostino, lost in his new and—to him—incredible thoughts, was unusually quiet. But later, after lunch, he was suddenly filled with an irresistible desire to go and spend time with the gang of boys. They had told him they would meet at Vespucci beach in the early afternoon to plan the day's excursions and exploits. After his initial feelings of repulsion and fear had passed, the brutal and humiliating company of the boys reasserted its dark appeal. He was in his room, lying on the bed, in the warm mottled shade of the lowered blinds. As was his habit, he was playing with the wooden pull switch of the electric light. From outside only a few noises entered: the turning wheels of a solitary carriage, dishes and glasses clattering in the street-side rooms of the pensione across the way. By contrast to the silence of the summer afternoon, the noises at home sounded sharper and more isolated. He could hear her enter the next room, her loud heels crossing the floor tiles. She walked back and forth, opening and shutting drawers, moving chairs around, touching objects. "Now she's going to take a nap," he thought for a moment, shaking himself from the torpor that had slowly come over him, "and then I won't be able to tell her I want to go to the beach." Worried, he got up from bed and left the room. His room opened onto the balcony facing the stairs. The mother's door was next to his. He walked up to it, but finding it slightly ajar, rather than knock as usual, he pushed the door softly until it was half open, guided perhaps unconsciously by his new desire to surprise his mother in her intimacy. In the mother's bedroom, much larger than his own, the bed was near the door, and facing the door was a chest of drawers topped by a wide mirror. The first thing he saw was his mother standing in front of the chest of drawers.

She wasn't naked, as he had almost sensed and hoped while entering, but rather partly undressed and in the act of removing her necklace and earrings in front of the mirror. She was wearing a sheer negligee that barely covered her hips. Beneath the two uneven and unbalanced swellings of her loins, one higher and contracted, the other lower and extended and relaxed, her elegant legs tapered in a listless pose from her long sturdy thighs all the way down to her calves and narrow heels. Her arms were raised to unhook the clasp of the necklace, lending her back a movement that could be seen through the transparent fabric, making the furrow that divided her expanse of tanned flesh blur and fade into two different backs, one lower and beneath the kidneys, the other higher and beneath the nape of the neck. Her armpits opened to the air like the jaws of two snakes, the soft long hairs like thin black tongues protruding as if eager to escape the heavy, sweaty constriction of her arms. Her whole large and splendid body seemed in Agostino's dazed eyes to sway and palpitate in the shadows of the room and, as if to leaven her nakedness, to expand immoderately, reabsorbing into the dilated, cloven roundness of her hips the legs along with the torso and head, and then to balloon, stretching and tapering upward, one extremity touching the floor and the other the ceiling. But in the mirror, in the mysterious shadow of a blackened painting, the pale and distant face seemed to look at him with inviting eyes and the mouth seemed to smile at him seductively.

Agostino's first impulse was to withdraw quickly, but a new thought, "She's a woman," immediately stopped him, his hand still on the door handle, his eyes wide open. He could feel the whole of his former filial spirit rebel against this paralysis and pull him away; but the new, timid yet strong spirit ruthlessly forced him to fix his reluctant eyes on a spot he would never have dared to set them the day before. So in the battle between repulsion and attraction, astonishment and pleasure, the details of the picture he was contemplating appeared more firm and sharp: the pose of the legs, the listlessness of the back, the profile of the armpits. They seemed to respond fully to the new feeling that required only this confirmation to overwhelm his imagination completely. Descending suddenly from respect and reverence to the opposite sentiments, he almost hoped that before his eyes her clumsiness would turn to vulgarity, her nudity to provocation, her innocence to naked guilt. His eyes shifted from astonishment to curiosity, filled with a scrutiny he considered almost scientific but whose false objectivity was related instead to the cruelty of their guiding sentiment. And while the blood rushed to his head, he kept repeating to himself, "She's a woman, nothing more than a woman," in words that seemed simultaneously to strike, disdain, and insult her back and legs.

The mother, having removed her necklace and set it on the marble top of the chest of drawers, brought her hands together at her earlobe in a graceful gesture to unscrew one of the earrings. Throughout this motion, she kept her head tilted to one side and turned toward the room. Agostino feared she would see him in the cheval glass situated near the window, in which he could see his whole body, upright and lurking, between the double doors. Forcing himself to remove his hand, he knocked lightly on the doorpost, asking, "May I?"

"Just a minute, dear," his mother said calmly. Agostino saw her move and disappear from sight. Then, after a quiet rustling, she reappeared in a long blue silk dressing gown.

"Mamma," said Agostino, without looking up, "I'm going to the beach."

"At this hour?" she said, distractedly. "But it's hot outside. Wouldn't it be better to take a short nap?" One hand reached out and caressed him on the cheek. With the other she smoothed a loose lock of his straight black hair from behind his neck.

Agostino said nothing, reverting to childhood for the occasion, and stood in stubborn silence, as he used to do whenever a request was not granted, eyes on the floor, chin lowered to his chest. This pose was well known to his mother, who interpreted it in her usual manner. "All right, then, if it matters to you so much," and added, "go ahead. But first go to the kitchen and have them give you a snack, but don't eat it right away, put it in the cabin, and above all don't go in the water before five. I should be there by then, and we can go for a swim together." These were her usual words of advice.

Agostino said nothing in reply and ran barefoot down the stone steps of the staircase. Behind him, he heard the door to her bedroom closing softly.

He raced down the stairs, slipped on his sandals in the entryway, opened the door, and went out into the street. He was immediately struck by a wall of torrid air, the silent ardor of the scorching August sun. At one end of the street, the sea glittered, motionless, beneath the distant, tremulous air. At the opposite end the red tree trunks of the pine grove tilted beneath the sultry green mass of their rounded foliage.

He hesitated, wondering whether it would be easier to go to the Vespucci beach along the water or through the pine grove. He decided on the beach because, although the sun beat down more heavily there, at least he wouldn't risk walking by it without noticing. He traveled the full length of the street to where it merged with the seashore, then he started to walk quickly, staying close to the walls.

He didn't realize it, but what attracted him to Vespucci, besides the company of the boys, was their brutal mocking of his mother and her alleged lovers. He could sense that his former affection was turning into an entirely different sentiment, both objective and cruel, and he felt he should seek out and cultivate the boys' heavy-handed irony for the simple fact that it had hastened this change. He couldn't say why he wanted so much to stop loving his mother, why he hated her love. Perhaps it was his resentment at being deceived and at having believed her to be so different from what she really was. Perhaps, since he couldn't love her without difficulty and insult, he preferred not to love her at all and to see her instead as merely a woman. He instinctively tried to free himself once and for all from the burden and shame of his former innocent, betrayed affection, which he now saw as little more than naïveté and foolishness. This was why the same cruel attraction that had made him stop and stare at his mother's back a few minutes earlier was now compelling him to seek out the brutal and humiliating company of the boys. Wasn't their irreverent talk—like his glimpse of her nudity—a way to destroy the filial condition he now found so repellent? A bitter pill that would either kill or cure him.

When he came within sight of Vespucci, he slowed his pace. Although his heart was beating rapidly and he was almost out of breath, he assumed an attitude of indifference. Saro was sitting under the tarp as usual, at his wobbly table with a flask of wine, a glass, and a bowl with the remains of a fish stew. No one else seemed to be around. Or rather, as he approached the tarp, he discovered, dark against the whiteness of the sand, little Homs, the black boy.

Saro didn't seem to be paying much attention to Homs. He was smoking a cigarette, lost in thought, a tattered old straw hat pulled over his eyes. "Where is everybody?" Agostino asked in a disappointed voice.

Saro looked up at him, regarded him for a moment, and said, "They all went to Rio." Rio was a deserted location up the coast, a few kilometers away, where a stream flowed into the sea between the sand and a canebrake.

"Oh," said Agostino, disappointed, "they went to Rio? What did they go there for?"

Homs replied, "They went to have lunch," and made an expressive gesture, bringing his hand to his mouth. But Saro shook his head and said, "You kids won't be happy till someone shoots you in the pants." The lunch was clearly a pretext to go steal fruit from the fields, at least as far as Agostino could tell.

"I didn't go," the black boy replied in a fawning voice, as if to ingratiate himself with Saro.

"You didn't go because they didn't want you," said Saro calmly.

The black boy protested, squirming in the sand. "No, I didn't go because I wanted to stay with you, Saro."

He had a smarmy, singsong voice. Saro said to him contemptuously, "Who gave you the right to call me by my first name, boy? We're not brothers, you know."

"No, we're not brothers," answered Homs, unperturbed. Indeed, he seemed jubilant, as if he were deeply pleased by the observation.

"So keep in your place," Saro concluded. Then he turned to Agostino. "They went to steal fruit and corn. That's their lunch."

"Are they coming back?" Agostino asked impatiently.

Saro said nothing. He looked at Agostino and seemed to be mulling something over. "They won't be back for a while," he replied slowly, "not before evening. But if we want, we can join them."

"How?"

"By boat," said Saro.

"Yes, let's take the boat," cried the black boy. Eager to go, he got up and stood next to Saro, but the man ignored him completely. "I've got a sailboat. In half an hour, more or less, we can be in Rio, if the wind is good."

"All right, let's go," said Agostino cheerfully. "But if they're in the fields, how are we going to find them?"

"Don't worry," said Saro, standing up and adjusting the black sash around his waist, "we'll find them." He turned toward Homs, who was peering at him anxiously, and added, "And you, boy, help me carry the sail and the mast."

"Right away, boss, right away," the black boy said jubilantly, following Saro into the shack.

Left to himself, Agostino stood up and looked around. The mistral wind had picked up, and the rippled sea was now a purplish blue. In a dust cloud of sun and sand, the shoreline between the sea and the grove appeared deserted as far as the eye could see. Agostino didn't know where Rio was, and with infatuated eyes he traced the capricious line of the solitary beach with all its points and bays. Where was Rio? Maybe over where the fury of the sun blurred sky, sea, and sand into a single widening haze? He was immensely attracted by the trip, and nothing in the world could make him miss it.

He was shaken from these reflections by the voices of the two coming out of the shack. Saro had a bundle of ropes and sails in one arm and a flask in the other. Behind him came the black boy, brandishing the green-and-white mast like a spear. "Off we go," said Saro, heading down the beach without a glance at Agostino. He seemed to be in an unusual hurry, Agostino didn't know why. He also noticed that his repellent flared nostrils seemed redder and more inflamed, as if the web of capillaries was suddenly swollen with thicker and brighter blood. "Off we go, off we go," sang the black boy in Saro's wake, the mast under his arm, improvising a kind of dance on the sand. Saro was ahead of him, almost to the cabins, so the black boy slowed down, waiting for Agostino to catch up. When he did, the black boy made a complicit gesture. Surprised, Agostino stopped.

"Listen up," said the black boy in a familiar tone, "I need to talk with Saro about some things, so do me a favor—don't come. Get lost."

"Why?" asked Agostino, surprised.

"I just told you, because I need to talk to Saro, just the two of us," the other boy said impatiently, stomping his foot.

"But I have to go to Rio," Agostino replied.

"You can go another time."

"No, I can't."

The black boy looked at him. In his blank eyes and oily,

quivering nostrils, Agostino sensed an anxious passion that repelled him. "Listen here, Pisa," he said, "if you don't come, I'll give you something you've never seen before." He let the mast slip from his hands and dug into his pockets, pulling out a slingshot made from a pine twig and two rubber bands tied together. "Nice, huh?" the black boy said, showing it to him.

But Agostino wanted to go to Rio, and Homs's insistence raised his suspicions. "No, I can't," he replied.

"Take the slingshot," the other boy said, looking for his hand and trying to force the object into his palm. "Take the slingshot and get lost."

"No," Agostino repeated, "I can't."

"I'll give you the slingshot and these playing cards," the black boy said. He dug into his pockets again and pulled out a small deck of pink cards with gilt edges. "Take both of them and get lost. You can use the slingshot to kill birds. The cards are new—"

"I said no," Agostino repeated.

The black boy looked at him, agitated and imploring. Large beads of sweat formed on his forehead, and his face suddenly twisted into a plaintive expression. "Why not?" he whined.

"I don't want to," said Agostino. And he fled toward the lifeguard, who by now had reached the boat on the beach. He heard the black boy yelling, "You'll be sorry," and, huffing and puffing, he reached Saro.

The boat was sitting on two raw pinewood logs, a short distance from the water. Saro had already tossed the sails into the boat and seemed impatient. "What's he doing?" he asked Agostino, pointing to the black boy.

"He'll be here in a second," said Agostino.

At that moment the black boy came running, the mast under his arm, making long leaps over the sand. Saro grabbed hold of the mast with the six fingers of his right hand and then with the six fingers of his left. He stood it upright and stuck it in a hole in the middle seat. Then he got into the boat, attached the tip of the sail, and pulled on the line; the sail slid up to the top of the mast. Saro turned to the black boy and said, "Now let's get to work."

Saro stood to the side of the boat, gripping one side of the bow. The black boy got ready to push the stern. Not knowing what to do, Agostino looked on. The boat was of medium size, half white and half green. On the bow, in black letters, you could read its name, *Amelia*. "Heave-ho!" said Saro. The boat slid over the logs, advancing across the sand. As soon as the hull rolled off the rear log, the black boy would squat down, pick it up, press it against his chest like a baby, and leaping over the sand as if in a modern dance, run to place it under the bow. "Heave-ho!" Saro repeated.

Again the boat slid forward a stretch, and again the black boy raced from stern to bow, skipping and jumping with the log in his arms. With a final push, the boat slid with its stern lower into the water and floated. Saro got into the boat and started slipping the oars into the oarlocks. At the same time, he gestured to Agostino, with a complicity that excluded the black boy, to climb on board. Agostino waded into the water up to his knees and started to climb in. He wouldn't have managed if the six fingers of Saro's right hand hadn't taken a firm hold of his arm and pulled him in like a cat. He looked up. While lifting him, Saro was concentrating not on him but on straightening out the left oar with his other hand. Filled with repulsion at the fingers that had gripped him, Agostino went to sit in the bow.

"Good boy," Saro said, "stay there. Now we're taking the boat out."

"Wait for me, I'm coming, too," shouted the black boy from the shore. Panting, he jumped into the water, nearing the boat and grabbing onto one side. But Saro said, "No, you're not coming."

"How am I supposed to get there?" the boy cried in distress. "How am I supposed to get there?"

"Take the streetcar," Saro replied, rowing vigorously from an upright position. "You'll get there before us."

"Why, Saro?" the boy insisted plaintively, running in the water beside the boat. "Why, Saro? I'm coming, too."

Without saying a word, Saro set the oars down, bent forward, and placed an enormous wide hand over the black boy's face. "I said you're not coming," he repeated calmly, and with a single thrust shoved the boy back into the water. "Why, Saro?" The boy continued to cry, "Why?" and his plaintive voice, amid the splashing of the water, sounded unpleasant to Agostino's ears, filling him with a vague pity. He looked at Saro, who smiled and said, "He's so annoying. What were we supposed to do?"

When the boat was farther from the shore. Agostino turned and saw the black boy emerging from the water and shaking his fist in a threatening gesture that seemed directed at him.

Without saying a word, Saro pulled the oars in and laid them on the bottom of the boat. He went toward the stern and tied the sail to the boom, stretching it out. The sail fluttered indecisively for a moment, as if the wind were battering it from both sides, then all of a sudden, it turned starboard with a loud snap, tightening and billowing out. Obediently, the boat also tilted starboard and started to skip over the light playful waves lifted by the mistral wind. "We're good," said Saro. "Now we can lie down and rest a while." He dropped down to the bottom of the boat and invited Agostino to join him. "If we sit on the bottom," he explained, "the boat goes faster." Agostino did the same and found himself sitting on the bottom of the boat, next to Saro.

The boat sailed smoothly despite its potbellied shape, tilting to one side, going up and down on the waves and occasionally rearing like a colt chafing at the bit. Saro was reclining with his head on the seat and one arm slipped below Agostino's neck to control the tiller. For a while he said nothing. "Do you go to school?" he finally asked.

Agostino looked at him. Lying on his back, Saro seemed to be voluptuously exposing his nose with its inflamed flared nostrils to the sea air, as if to refresh them. His mouth was half open beneath his mustache, his eyes half closed. Through his unbuttoned shirt you could see the hairs, gray and dirty, rustling on his chest. "Yes," said Agostino, with a shiver of unexpected fear.

"What year are you in?"

"The third year of middle school."

"Give me your hand," said Saro, and before Agostino could refuse, he grabbed hold of it. Agostino felt like he was trapped not by a hand but by a snare. The six short stubby fingers covered his hand, circled it, and joined below it. "And what do they teach you," Saro continued, getting into a better position and sinking into a sort of bliss.

"Latin . . . Italian . . . geography . . . history," Agostino stuttered.

"Do they teach you poetry, any nice poems?" Saro asked in a soft voice.

"Yes," said Agostino, "they also teach us poetry."

"Tell me one."

The boat reared up, and Saro, without moving or modifying his blissful pose, gave the tiller a shove. "Uh, I don't know," said Agostino, frightened and embarrassed, "they teach me lots of poems. Carducci..."

"Ah, yes, Carducci..." Saro repeated mechanically. "Tell me a poem by Carducci."

"*By the Sources of Clitumnus*," Agostino proposed, horrified at the hand that would not release its grip and trying slowly but surely to break it.

"Yes, *By the Sources of Clitumnus*," Saro said in a dreamy voice.

With an unsteady voice, Agostino began:

"Still, Clitumnus, down from the mountains, dark with
Waving ash trees, where 'mid the branches perfumed..."[1]

The boat skipped along, Saro was still on his back, nose to the wind, eyes closed, making gestures with his head as if he were scanning the verses. Suddenly clinging to the poem as if it were the only means of avoiding a conversation he sensed would be compromising and dangerous, Agostino continued to recite slowly and clearly. All the while he tried to free his hand from the six fingers clutching it, but the grip was tighter than ever. He was terrified to realize that the end of the poem was approaching, so to the last stanza of *By the Sources of Clitumnus* he appended the first line of "Before San Guido." It was also a test, as if he needed one,

---

1. G. L. Bickersteth, *Carducci: A Selection of His Poems, with Verse Translations, Notes, and Three Introductory Essays* (London, New York, Bombay and Calcutta: Longmans, Green, and Co., 1913).

to confirm that Saro didn't really care about poetry and had another very different purpose in mind. What exactly that was he could not quite understand. And the test was successful. "The cypresses which still to Bolgheri run stately and tall . . ." sounded jarring, but Saro gave no indication he had noticed the change. So Agostino interrupted his recital and said in exasperation, "Would you please let go?" while trying to free himself.

Saro was startled, and without letting go he opened his eyes, turned, and looked at Agostino. In the boy's face there must have been such wild-eyed repulsion, such barely concealed terror, that Saro seemed to realize immediately that his plan had failed. Slowly, finger by finger, he released Agostino's aching hand and said in a low voice, as if he were speaking to himself, "What are you afraid of? Now I'm going to bring you to shore."

He pulled himself up heavily and gave a push to the tiller. The boat turned toward the shore.

Without saying a word, Agostino got up from the bottom of the boat, rubbing his aching hand, and went to sit in the bow. As they approached the shore, he could see the whole beach, which was quite wide at that point, and its white, deserted, sun-beaten sand. Beyond it, the pine grove was thicker, tilting, purplish. Rio was a V-shaped crevice in the dunes. Farther up, the reeds formed a blue-green smudge. But in front of Rio, he noticed a group of figures gathered from whose midst a wisp of black smoke rose to the sky. He turned to Saro, who was sitting in the stern adjusting the tiller with one hand, and asked, "Is that where we're landing?"

"Yes, that's Rio," Saro replied indifferently.

As the boat approached the shore, Agostino saw the

group around the fire suddenly break up and run toward them. He realized it was the gang. He saw them waving. They must have been shouting something, but the wind carried their voices away. "Is it them?" he asked anxiously.

"Yes, it's them," Saro said.

The boat got closer and closer to shore and Agostino could discern the boys clearly. No one was missing: Tortima, Berto, Sandro, and all the others were there. And in a discovery he found unpleasant, though he didn't know why, so was Homs. Like the others, he was jumping up and down and shouting by the water.

The boat sailed straight to the beach, then Saro gave a shove to the tiller, turning it sideways. Rushing at the sail, he gathered it in his arms, shortened it, and lowered it. The boat rocked from one side to the other in the shallow water. From the deck of the boat Saro picked up an anchor and threw it overboard. "We're getting out," he said. He climbed out of the boat and waded through the water to the boys waiting for him on the shore.

Agostino saw them crowding around and applauding, which Saro welcomed with a shake of the head. Another louder round of applause greeted his own arrival, and for a moment he fooled himself into believing it was friendly and polite. He realized immediately that he was wrong. Everyone was laughing, sarcastic, and contemptuous. Berto shouted, "So, our little Pisa likes to go on boat rides," and Tortima made a face, bringing his hand to his mouth. The others echoed their behavior. Even Sandro, usually so reserved, seemed to view him with contempt. Homs, instead, was leaping around Saro, who walked on ahead toward the fire the boys had lit on the beach. Shocked and vaguely alarmed, Agostino went with the others to sit by the fire.

The boys had packed wet sand into a kind of makeshift pit. Pinecones, pine needles, and brush were on the fire. Laid across the mouth of the pit, a dozen ears of corn were slowly roasting. Nearby you could see, on top of a newspaper, a big watermelon and clusters of fruit. "What a good boy, little Pisa," Berto started up again after they were sitting down, "now you and Homs can be buddies. Sit a little closer to each other. You're, how can I put it? You're brothers. He's dark, you're white, otherwise there's no difference. You both like going for boat rides."

The black boy snickered contentedly. Saro, huddled over, was busy turning the ears of corn on the fire. The others were snickering. Berto was the most derisive of all, shoving Agostino into the black boy so hard that for a moment they were on top of each other, one snickering at his abasement as if it were flattery, the other uncomprehending and filled with repulsion. "I don't understand you guys," Agostino blurted out, "I went for a boat ride. What's wrong with that?"

"Oh, what's wrong with that? He went for a boat ride. What's wrong with that?" many voices repeated, ironically. Some of the boys were holding their bellies from laughter.

"Yeah, what's wrong with it?" Berto repeated in the same tone of voice. "Nothing at all. On the contrary, Homs thinks everything's right about it. Don't you, Homs?"

The black boy agreed, jubilantly. The truth finally began to dawn on Agostino, however vaguely. He couldn't help but establish a connection between the teasing and Saro's strange behavior during the trip. "I don't know what you mean," he declared. "I didn't do anything wrong during the boat ride. Saro made me recite some poetry, that's all."

"Oh, oh, poetry," he heard the cries from all around.

"Saro, tell them I'm not lying," Agostino cried, turning red in the face.

Saro said neither yes nor no, settling for a smile and sneaking what one might call a curious glance in his direction. The boys interpreted his seemingly indifferent but in fact treacherous and self-serving behavior as a contradiction of Agostino. "Of course," many voices repeated, "ask the innkeeper if the wine is good, right, Saro? Nice try. Oh, Pisa, Pisa."

The vindictive black boy seemed to be enjoying this more than anyone. Agostino turned to him and, trembling with rage, abruptly asked, "What's so funny?"

"Why nothing," said Homs, stepping aside.

"Hey, don't fight, Saro will make peace between you," Berto said. But the boys were already talking about something else, as if what they had been alluding to was moot and no longer worth mentioning. They talked about how they had snuck into a field and stolen the corn and fruit. About how they had seen the farmer chase after them, armed and furious. About how they had fled and the farmer had fired his gun at them without striking anyone. The ears of corn were ready, browned and roasted on the embers. Saro removed them from the grate and, with his usual paternal complacency, distributed them to everyone. Agostino took advantage of a moment when everyone was intent on eating, and with a somersault made his way to Sandro, who off to one side was nibbling at his corn.

"I don't understand," he started. The other boy gave him a knowing look, and Agostino realized there was no need to say more. "Homs came on the streetcar," Sandro uttered slowly, "and he said you and Saro had gone for a boat ride."

"What's wrong with that?"

"Keep me out of it," replied Sandro with his eyes to the ground, "it's between you two, you and the black boy. But as for Saro..." He let the sentence drift off and stared at Agostino.

"As for Saro?"

"Well, let's just say that I wouldn't go on a boat ride with Saro."

"Why not?"

Sandro looked around them and then, lowering his voice, he gave Agostino the explanation he had almost intuited without fully understanding. "Oh," said Agostino. And without being able to say more, he returned to the group.

Squatting among the boys, with his cold good-natured head leaning on one shoulder, Saro was the very picture of a good father surrounded by his children. But now Agostino couldn't look at him without a deep and even stronger hatred than he felt toward the black boy. What was particularly despicable about Saro was his silence in the face of Agostino's protests, as if to insinuate that the things the boys had accused him of really had taken place. Yet he couldn't help but perceive the contempt and derision that separated him from the others. The same distance, now that he noticed, between the gang and the black boy. Except that the black boy, rather than feel humiliated and offended like Agostino, seemed to be amused by it. More than once he tried to talk about the subject burning inside him, but he was met with ridicule and apathy. Besides, although Sandro's explanation couldn't have been clearer, Agostino still couldn't fully understand what had happened. Everything was obscure both in and around him, as if rather than the sunlit beach, sky, and sea, there were only shadows, fog, and vague menacing shapes.

In the meantime the boys had finished devouring the roasted corn and thrown the cobs away in the sand. "Should we go for a swim in Rio?" one of them proposed, and the proposal was instantly accepted. Even Saro, who was supposed to bring them all back to the Vespucci beach in his boat later, stood up and came with them.

Walking along the beach, Sandro broke away from the group and joined Agostino. "You're mad at the black kid," he whispered, "so scare him a little."

"How?" asked Agostino, downcast.

"Beat him up."

"He's stronger than me," said Agostino, remembering their arm wrestling, "but if you help me—"

"What's it got to do with me? This is between you and him." Sandro said these words with a special tone, as if to insinuate that his thoughts as to why Agostino despised Homs were no different than everyone else's. Agostino felt his heart pierced by a profound bitterness. Even Sandro— the only one who had shown him any friendship so far— also participated in and believed the slander. Having offered this advice, Sandro walked away from Agostino and joined the others, as if he were afraid of being near him. From the beach they now passed through the undergrowth of young pines. Then they crossed a sandy path and entered into the canebrake. The reeds were dense, and many of them had feathery white plumes on top. The boys appeared and disappeared between the tall green stalks, slipping on the cane sap and shaking the canes with a dry rustling of the stiff fibrous leaves. They finally found a point where the canebrake opened up to a small muddy riverbank. When the boys appeared, big frogs leapt from all around into the glassy compact water. And here, one leaning against the

other, they started undressing before the narrowed eyes of
Saro who, sitting on a rock close to the reeds, seemed intent
on smoking but was spying on them. Agostino was embarrassed, but fearing more teasing, he, too, began to loosen
his trousers, as slowly as possible, casting furtive glances at
the others. But the boys seemed overjoyed to get naked and
tore off their clothes, bumping into one another and joking
around. Against the green background of the cane, their
bodies were brown and white, a miserable, hairy white from
their groins to their bellies. This whiteness revealed something strangely deformed, ungainly, and overly muscular
about their bodies, typical of manual laborers. The only
one who didn't actually seem naked was Sandro, blond in
the groin and on the head, graceful and well proportioned,
perhaps because his whole body was evenly tanned. Not
naked, that is, in the foul manner of kids at a public
swimming pool. The boys, getting ready to dive in, acted
out hundreds of obscene gestures, tripping, pushing, and
touching each other with brashness and an unrestrained
promiscuity that shocked Agostino, who was new to this
type of thing. He too was naked, his feet bare and caked
with cold mud, but he would have preferred to hide behind
the cane, if only to escape the looks cast his way through
the half-closed eyes of Saro, crouching and motionless, like
a giant toad who dwelled in the canebrake. Except, as usual,
Agostino's repulsion was weaker than the murky attraction
that drew him to the gang. So thoroughly intermingled
were the two that he couldn't tell how much pleasure was
actually concealed by his loathing. The boys measured each
other up, boasting of their virility and physique. Tortima
was the most vain and at the same time the most brawny,
the most deformed, the most plebian and sordid of the

group. He got so excited that he shouted to Agostino, "What if I were to show up one nice morning at your mother's, naked as the day, what do you think she'd say? Would she come with me?"

"No," Agostino said.

"And I say she would, immediately," said Tortima. "She'd look me up and down, just to size me up, and then she'd say, 'Come on, Tortima, let's have some fun.'"

All this horseplay made everyone laugh. At the sound of, "Come on, Tortima, let's have some fun," they all jumped into the stream, one after the other, diving in headfirst like the frogs who had been disturbed by their arrival a short while earlier.

The bank was surrounded by reeds so tall they could only see one stretch of the river. But from the middle of the current, they could see the whole stream which, with the imperceptible movement of its dark dense waters, flowed into the sea farther downstream, between the sandbanks. Upstream the river flowed between two rows of short fat silvery bushes that cast fluttering shadows over the reflecting water. In the distance a small iron bridge against a background of cane and poplar trees, dense and pressed tightly together, completed the landscape. A red house, half hidden between the trees, seemed to stand watch over the bridge.

For a moment Agostino felt happy as he swam while the cold powerful stream tugged at his legs, and he forgot every hurt and every wrong. The boys were swimming in all directions, their heads and arms breaking through the smooth green surface. Their voices echoed clearly in the still air. Through the glassy transparency of the water, their bodies looked like white offshoots of plants that, rising to the surface from the darkness below, moved whichever way the current took them. He swam up to Berto, who was nearby, and asked, "Are there a lot of fish in this river?"

Berto looked at him and said, "What are you doing here? Why don't you keep Saro company?"

"I like swimming," Agostino replied, feeling hurt, and turned and swam away.

But he wasn't as strong and experienced as the others. Tiring quickly, he let the current carry him toward the mouth of the stream. Soon the boys with their shouting and splashing were far behind him. The canebrake thinned, and the water turned clearer and colorless, revealing the sandy bottom covered with wavy gray ripples. After passing a deeper pool, a kind of green eye in the diaphanous current, he placed his feet on the sand and, struggling against the force of the water, climbed out on the bank. The stream flowed into the sea, swirling and forming almost an upswell of water. Losing its compactness, the current fanned out, thinning, becoming little more than a liquid veil over the smooth sands. The sea flowed into the river in light foam-tipped ripples. Here and there pools forgotten by the current reflected the bright sky in the squishy untrodden sand. Completely naked, Agostino walked for a while on the soft gleaming sand, amusing himself by pressing his feet down hard and watching the water instantly rise up to flood his footprints. He was feeling a vague, desperate desire to cross the river and disappear down the shore, leaving behind the boys, Saro, his mother, and his whole former life. Who knows if by walking straight ahead, along the sea, on the soft white sand, he wouldn't reach a land where none of these awful things existed. A land where he would be welcomed as his heart desired and be able to forget everything he had learned, and then relearn it without shame or offense, in the sweet and natural way that had to exist and of which he had a dark presentiment. He looked at the haze on the horizon enveloping the ends of the sea, the beach, and the woods, and he felt drawn to that immensity as if it were the only thing that could release him from his servitude. The shouts of the boys, heading across the beach toward the boat, awakened him from these sad imaginings. One boy was shaking Agostino's clothes in the air. Berto shouted, "Pisa, we're leaving." He shook himself and, walking along the shore, reached the gang.

All the boys crowded together in the shallow water. Saro was busy warning them paternally that the boat was too small to hold everyone, but he was obviously joking. Like madmen, they threw themselves at the boat, shouting, twenty hands grabbing at the sides, and in the blink of an eye the boat was crammed with their gesticulating bodies. Some lay down on the floor. Others piled up in the stern near the tiller. Others took the bow, and yet others took the seats. Lastly some sat on the edges, letting their legs dangle in the water. The boat really was too small for so many people and the water came almost all the way up the sides.

"So everybody's here," said Saro, filled with good humor. Standing up, he unfurled the sail, and the boat glided out to sea. The boys saluted the departure with applause.

But Agostino didn't share their good humor. He thought he spied an opportunity to clear his name and be exonerated from the slander weighing on him. He took advantage of a moment when the boys were arguing to approach Homs, who was alone, perched in the bow, looking in his blackness like a new style of figurehead. Squeezing his arm tightly he asked, "Listen here, what did you go around telling everyone about me?"

He had chosen the wrong moment, but it was the first opportunity Agostino had found to approach the black boy who, aware of Agostino's hostility, had kept his distance the whole time they were on land. "I told the truth," Homs said, without looking at him.

"What do you mean?"

The black boy uttered a sentence that frightened Agostino. "Don't press me, I only told the truth, but if you keep pitting Saro against me, I'm going to go tell your mother everything. Watch out, Pisa."

"What?" exclaimed Agostino, feeling the abyss opening beneath his feet. "What are you talking about? Are you crazy? I . . . I . . ." he stuttered, unable to put into words the lurid image that had suddenly materialized before him. But he didn't have time to continue. The whole boat had erupted in laughter.

"Look at the two of them, one next to the other," repeated Berto, laughing. "We should have a camera to take a picture of the two of them together, Homs and Pisa. Stay where you are, lovebirds." His face burning with shame, Agostino turned and saw everybody laughing. Even Saro was snickering beneath his mustache, his eyes half closed behind the smoke from his cigar. Recoiling as if he had touched a reptile, Agostino broke away from the black boy, pulled his knees to his chest, and stared at the sea through eyes brimming with tears.

It was late and the sun had set, cloudy and red on the horizon above a violet sea riddled with sharp glassy lights. The boat was moving as best it could in the gusts that had suddenly risen, and all the boys on board made it tilt dangerously to one side. The bow was turned toward the open sea and seemed to be headed not for land but for the faint outlines of faraway islands that rose from the swollen sea, like mountains above a plateau. Holding between his legs the watermelon stolen by the boys, Saro split it with his sailor's knife and cut it into thick slices that he distributed to the gang paternally. The boys passed them around and ate greedily, taking big bites, digging their teeth in or breaking off big chunks of the flesh with their fingers. Then, one after the other, the white-and-green rinds were tossed overboard into the sea. After the watermelon, out came the flask of wine, which Saro pulled solemnly from below deck. The flask made the rounds, and Agostino also had to take a swig. The wine was strong and warm and went right to his head. Once the empty flask had been stowed, Tortima started singing an obscene song, and everyone joined in on the refrain. Between the stanzas, the boys urged Agostino to sing along. Everyone could tell he was miserable, but no one spoke with him except to tease and make fun of him. Agostino's sense of oppression and silent pain was made more bitter and unbearable by the fresh wind on the sea and the magnificent blazing of the sunset over the violet waters. He found it utterly unjust that on such a sea, beneath such a sky, a boat like theirs should be so full of spite, cruelty, and malicious corruption. A boat overflowing with boys acting like monkeys, gesticulating and obscene, helmed by the blissful and bloated Saro, created between the sea and sky a sad unbelievable vision. There were moments he hoped it would sink. He thought he would gladly die, so infected did he feel by their impurity and so ruined. Distant was the morning hour when he had first seen the red tarp on Vespucci beach; distant and belonging, it seemed, to an age gone by. Every time the boat climbed a big wave, the gang gave a shout that made him jump. Every

time the black boy spoke to him with his repellent, deceitful, and servile deference, he retreated farther into the bow
to avoid hearing him. The dark realization came to him
that a difficult and miserable age had begun for him, and he
couldn't imagine when it would end. The boat drifted for a
while in the sea, making it almost to the harbor and then
turning back. As soon as they came ashore, Agostino raced
away without saying goodbye to anyone. But then he slowed
his step. Turning back, he could see in the distance, on the
darkening beach, the boys helping Saro pull the boat onto
dry land.

3

AFTER that day a dark and tormented period began for Agostino. On that day his eyes had been forced open, but what he learned was far more than he could bear. What oppressed and embittered him was not so much the novelty as the quality of the things he had come to know, their massive and undigested importance. He had thought, for example, that after those revelations, his relations with his mother would have been settled, and the unease, irritation, and repulsion that her caresses provoked in him, especially in recent days, would be almost magically resolved and appeased by a new and serene awareness. But this did not happen. His irritation, unease, and repulsion persisted. While before they were signs of a son's affection, tainted and troubled by the dark awareness of his mother's womanhood, now, after the morning spent under Saro's tarp, they stemmed from an acrid, impure curiosity that his continued respect for family made intolerable. While before he had struggled in the dark to free that affection from an unjustified repulsion, now he felt almost obliged to separate his rational new knowledge from the promiscuous, visceral sense that he was born of a person he wanted to see only as a woman. He felt as if all his unhappiness would vanish on the day he could see in his mother the same beautiful creature perceived by Saro and the boys. And he searched doggedly for occasions that would confirm this conviction, only to find that he had replaced his former reverence with cruelty and his affection with sensuality.

At home his mother, as in the past, did not conceal herself from his gaze, nor did she notice any change in it. Agostino felt as if she were provoking and pursuing him with her maternal immodesty. Sometimes he would hear her calling him and find her at her vanity, in dishabille, her breasts half naked. Or he would wake up and see her leaning over him for a morning kiss, allowing her dressing gown to fall open and her body's outlines to appear through the transparency of her light, wrinkled negligee. She walked back and forth in front of him as if he weren't there. She would pull her stockings on and off, slip into her clothes, dab on some perfume, apply her makeup. All of these gestures, which had once seemed so natural to Agostino, now seemed to take on meaning and become an almost visible part of a larger, more dangerous reality, dividing his spirit between curiosity and pain. He repeated to himself "She's only a woman" with the objective indifference of a connoisseur. But one moment later, unable to bear his mother's unawareness or his own attentions, he wanted to shout, "Cover yourself, stop showing yourself to me, I'm not who I used to be." Anyway, his hopes to see his mother only as a woman failed almost immediately. He realized quickly that, although she was now a woman in his eyes, she remained more a mother than ever. And he realized that the sense of cruel shame, which he had briefly attributed to the novelty of his feelings, would never leave him. He suddenly grasped that she would always be the person he had loved with pure and unencumbered affection; that she would always mix with her most womanly gestures the affectionate acts that for so long had been the only ones he knew; that he would never be able to separate his new perception of her from the wounded memory of her former dignity.

He did not doubt that his mother and the young boatman were engaged in the type of relations that the boys had described under Saro's tarp. And he was strangely amazed by the change that had taken place in himself. His heart had been filled with jealousy of his mother and dislike of the young man, two vague and almost dormant feelings. But now, in the effort to remain calm and objective, he would have liked to feel understanding toward the young man and indifference toward his mother—except his understanding was little more than complicity, and his indifference indiscretion. Rarely did he accompany them out to sea anymore, always finding a way to escape the invitations. But every time he did go with them, Agostino realized he was studying the young man's behavior and words, as if waiting for him to overstep the boundaries of his usual urbane gallantry; likewise, he studied the mother's actions, as if hoping to see his suspicions confirmed. These sentiments were unbearable for him because they were the exact opposite of what he desired. And he almost missed the compassion he used to feel for his mother's clumsiness, so much more human and affectionate than his cruel attention to her now.

From those days spent struggling with himself, he was left with a murky sense of impurity. He felt as if he had bartered away his former innocence, not for the virile, serene condition he had aspired to but rather for a confused hybrid state in which, without any form of recompense, the old repulsions were compounded by the new. What was the use of seeing things clearly if the only thing clarity brought was a new and deeper darkness? Sometimes he wondered how older boys, knowing what he knew, could still love their mothers. He concluded that this awareness must have gradually killed their filial affection, while in him one had not succeeded in expelling the other, and their coexistence had created a turbulent mix.

As can happen, the place of these discoveries and conflicts—his home—soon became unbearable. At least when he was on the beach, he was distracted and numbed by the sun, the crowd of bathers, and the presence of so many other women. But at home, between four walls, alone with his mother, he felt prey to every temptation, trapped by every contradiction. On the beach the mother blended into all the other naked flesh, while at home she appeared singular and excessive. Like a private theater in which the actors seem larger than life, her every action and word stood out. Agostino had a sharp and adventurous sense of family privacy. As a child he had seen the halls, closets, and rooms as strange mutable places to make the most curious discoveries and live out the most fantastic adventures. But now, after the encounter with the boys under the red tarp, those events and discoveries belonged to a realm so different that he couldn't tell whether they attracted or frightened him. He used to imagine ambushes, shadows, presences, voices in the furniture and in the walls. But now, rather than the fictions of his boyish exuberance, his imagination focused on the new reality that seemed to permeate the walls, the furnishings, and even the air of the house. The innocent fervor that his mother's kisses and trusting sleep used to calm at night was replaced by the burning, shameful indiscretion that was magnified in the dead of night and seemed to feed his impure fire. Everywhere he went in the house he detected the signs, the traces, of a woman, the only one he happened to be near, and that woman was his mother. When he was close to her, he felt as if he was monitoring her, when he approached her door it was as if he were spying on her. And when he touched her clothes he felt as if he was touching the woman who had worn them against her skin. At night he conjured up the most troubling nightmares. Sometimes he felt like the child he used to be, frightened of every noise and shadow, the child who would suddenly get up and run to the safety of his mother's bed. But the instant he set his feet on the floor, even amid the confusion of the dream, he realized that his fear was nothing more than a maliciously disguised curiosity and that, once he was in his mother's arms, his nocturnal visit would quickly reveal its true, hidden purpose. Or he would suddenly wake up and wonder whether the young boatman chanced to be on the other side of the wall, in the next room, with his mother. Certain sounds seemed to confirm this suspicion. Others allayed it. For a while he would toss and turn in his bed and then, without knowing how he arrived there, find himself in his nightshirt, in the hall outside his mother's door, in the act of listening and spying. Once he even yielded to temptation and entered without knocking. He stood in the middle of the room without moving. Through the open window the moonlight shone, indirect and white, and his eyes focused on the bed where the dark hair and long bulging shapes wrapped in the sheets revealed the woman's presence. "Is that you, Agostino?" the mother asked, roused from her sleep. Without saying a word, he quickly returned to his room.

His repulsion at being near his mother led him to spend more and more time at Vespucci beach. But the other, different torments that awaited him there made it no less hateful than home. The boys' attitude toward him after the boat ride with Saro had not changed. Indeed, it had taken on a definitive aspect, as if based on unshakable conviction and judgment. He was the boy who had accepted that fatal, notorious invitation from Saro, and nothing would change their minds. So their initial envious contempt motivated by his wealth was compounded by a scorn based on his supposed deviance. In a sense, to their brutish minds, the one seemed to explain, to give rise to the other. He was rich, they insinuated through their cruel, humiliating behavior—was it any wonder he was deviant as well? Agostino quickly discovered how close the correlation between the two accusations was, and he came to the vague realization that this was the price he had to pay for being different and superior: a social superiority that was displayed in his finer clothing, his talk about the comforts of his home, his tastes, his speech; a moral superiority that drove him to reject allegations of his relations with Saro, and that constantly appeared in his obvious loathing for the boys' behavior and manners. Consequently, more to express the humiliating state in which he found himself than out of conscious desire, he decided to be the person he thought they wanted him to be, one identical to them. He deliberately started wearing his ugliest and most worn-out clothes, to the great dismay of his mother, who no longer recognized in him any sign of his former vanity. He deliberately stopped talking about his house and his wealth. He deliberately pretended to appreciate and enjoy the behavior and manners that still horrified him. Worse still, and after a painful struggle, one day when they were teasing him, as usual, about his ride with Saro, he deliberately said that he was tired of denying the truth, that the things they were saying about him really had happened, and that he had no problem telling them about it. These assertions startled Saro, but he carefully avoided contradicting them, perhaps out of fear of exposing himself. This open acknowledgment that the rumors which had tormented him were true initially created great amazement, since the boys didn't expect such boldness from someone so timid and bashful. But then a torrent of indiscreet questions followed about what had actually happened, and these completely overwhelmed him; flustered and upset, he refused to say another word. The boys interpreted his silence in their own way, of course, as the silence of shame rather than what it really was: ignorance and the inability to lie. And the brunt of their usual teasing and contempt grew even worse.

Despite this failure, however, he really had changed. More from his daily association with them than by any act of will, he had grown more like the boys without realizing it, or rather, he had lost his former pleasures without managing to acquire any new ones. More than once, when he'd had enough, he avoided Vespucci beach and sought out the simple companions and innocent games of Speranza beach with which his summer had begun. But there was something so bland about the polite children who awaited him there; their amusements ruled by parents' warnings and nannies' supervision were so boring, their talk of school, stamp collections, adventure books, and other such things, so insipid. The truth was that the camaraderie of the gang, their foul language, their talk about women, stealing from the fields, and even their violence and harsh treatment of him had transformed him and made him adverse to the old friendships. Something that happened during that period confirmed his belief. One morning, arriving later than usual at Vespucci beach, he found neither Saro, who was off doing errands, nor the gang. Despondent, he sat down on a boat by the water. While he was staring at the beach, hoping that at least Saro would appear, he was approached by a man and a boy who was perhaps two years younger than Agostino. The man was short with fat stubby legs beneath a protruding belly and a round face with a pince-nez clamped to a pointed nose. He looked like an office worker or a teacher. The pale skinny boy, wearing bathing trunks a couple of sizes too large, was hugging to his chest an enormous, brand-new leather soccer ball. Holding his son by the arm, the man came up to Agostino and looked at him for a while, undecided. Finally he asked if they couldn't go for a boat ride. "Of course you can," replied Agostino without hesitation.

The man looked at him skeptically, peering over his eyeglasses, and then asked how much an hour would cost. Agostino knew the fares and told him. Then he realized the man had mistaken him for the boatman's son or helper, which somehow flattered him. "All right, let's go," the man said.

Without a second thought, Agostino took the raw pine log that served as a roller and placed it under the stern of the boat. Then, grabbing hold of the corners with both hands, in an effort redoubled by a strange surge of pride, he pushed the boat into the water. After helping the boy and his father climb in, he jumped aboard himself and took command of the oars.

For a little while, on the calm and deserted early-morning sea, Agostino rowed without saying a word. The boy hugged the ball to his chest and looked at Agostino with a wan expression. The man, seated awkwardly, his belly between his legs, twisted his head around on a fat neck and appeared to be enjoying the landscape. Finally he asked Agostino whether he was the boatman's son or helper. Agostino replied that he was the helper. "And how old are you?" the man inquired.

"Thirteen," said Agostino.

"You see," said the man to his son, "this boy is almost the same age as you and he's already working." Then, to Agostino, "Do you go to school?"

"I wish … but how can I?" replied Agostino, taking on the deceitful tone he had often heard the boys in the gang adopt to address similar questions. "I gotta make a living, mister."

"You see," the father turned to his son again, "this boy can't go to school because he has to work, and you have the nerve to complain because you have to study?"

"We're a big family," continued Agostino, rowing vigorously, "and we all work."

"And how much can you make in a day?" the man asked.

"It depends," replied Agostino. "If a lot of people come, as much as twenty or thirty lire."

"Which you naturally give to your father," the man interrupted.

"Of course," Agostino replied without hesitation. "Except for tips, of course."

The man didn't feel like holding up this particular remark to his son as an example, but he made a grave nod of approval. The son was quiet, hugging the ball to his chest more tightly and looking at Agostino with dull, watery eyes.

"How would you like to have a leather ball like this for yourself, boy?" the man suddenly asked Agostino.

Agostino already had two soccer balls, and they had long been sitting in his bedroom, discarded along with his other playthings. But he said, "Yes, I would like that, of course, but how could we manage? We have to take care of basics first."

The man turned toward his son and, more to tease, it seemed, than to express his actual intentions, said to him, "Come on, Piero, give your ball to this poor boy who doesn't have one." The son looked at the father, then at Agostino, and with an almost jealous vehemence hugged the ball to his chest without saying a word. "You don't want to?" the father asked softly. "Why not?"

"It's mine," the boy said.

"Don't worry," Agostino interjected at this point with a phony smile, "it'd be no use to me anyway. I don't have any time to play, but he . . ."

The father smiled at these words, pleased to have presented a moral example to his son in the flesh and blood. "You see, this boy is better than you," he added, patting his son on the head. "He's poor and he still doesn't want your ball. He's letting you keep it, but every time you start acting up and complaining, I want you to remember that in the world there are boys like this who have to work for a living and have never had a soccer ball or any other plaything."

"It's my ball," the son replied, obstinate.

"Yes, it's yours." The father sighed distractedly. He looked at his watch and said, "Let's head back, boy," in a changed and domineering voice. Without saying a word, Agostino turned the boat toward the shore.

As they came close to the beach, he saw Saro standing in the water observing his maneuvers, and he was afraid the boatman would embarrass him by revealing the trick he had played. But Saro didn't open his mouth. Perhaps he understood. Perhaps he didn't care. Quietly and solemnly, he helped Agostino pull the boat onto the beach. "This is for you," said the man, giving Agostino the agreed sum plus something extra. Agostino took the money and brought it to Saro. "But this part I'm keeping for myself. It's the tip," he added with smug and deliberate impudence. Saro didn't say a word. With a crooked smile he put the money in the black sash around his waist and walked away slowly across the sand toward the shack.

This small incident left Agostino with the feeling once and for all that he no longer belonged to the world of children like the boy with the soccer ball, and that, anyway, he had sunk so low that he could no longer live without deceit and vexation. But it pained him not to be like the boys in the gang either. There was still too much delicacy in him. If he were like them, he sometimes thought, he wouldn't be so hurt by their crudeness, their vulgarity, their bluntness. So he found that he had lost his original identity without acquiring through his loss another.

lack of identity

4

On a late-summer day, Agostino and the boys in the gang went to the pine grove to hunt for birds and mushrooms. Of their various feats and exploits, this was the one he liked best. They entered the grove and walked for a long time on the soft soil through a natural corridor formed by the red columns of tree trunks, looking toward the sky to see whether high above them, between the towering branches, there was anything moving or stirring between the pines. When there was, Berto, Tortima, or Sandro, the best of the three, would pull back the rubber band of his slingshot and shoot a sharp rock at the spot where he thought he saw movement. Sometimes a sparrow would plummet to the ground, its wing shattered. Fluttering and chirping pitifully, it would hop and flail about until one of the boys grabbed it and crushed its head between his fingers. But the boys usually caught nothing and had to content themselves with long wanderings through the dense grove, their heads tilted back and their eyes staring upward, venturing farther and deeper to where the underbrush between the pine trees started and the soft barren ground of the dried pine needles gave way to a tangle of thornbushes. This was where the mushroom picking began. It had rained for a couple of days, and the underbrush was still damp with resin-coated leaves and marshy green soil. Amid the thickest bushes, there were large yellow mushrooms as well as small clusters of tiny ones, lustrous with mucous and moisture. The boys picked them delicately, poking their arms between the briars, sliding two fingers beneath the caps and pulling up carefully so they would also get the dirt- and moss-covered stems. Then they stuck them one by one on long pointed sticks. As they worked their way from thicket to thicket, they gathered a few pounds—dinner for Tortima who, as the strongest boy, confiscated the day's haul for himself. The harvest was bountiful, for after a long hike they found a virgin patch, so to speak, where the mushrooms sprouted densely, one beside the other, on a bed of moss. By sundown the patch had still been only half explored, but it was late and, with several skewers of mushrooms and two or three birds, the boys slowly made their way home.

Usually they took a path that led straight to the beach, but that day they chased after a sparrow that kept taunting them, flitting between the lowest branches of the pine trees and constantly fooling them into thinking it would be an easy target. So they ended up crossing the full length of the grove whose easternmost tip encroached on an area almost abutting the houses of the town. It was growing dark by the time they emerged from the last pine trees into the piazza of a neighborhood on the outskirts of town. The immense unpaved piazza was covered with sand, scattered piles of debris, and tufts of thistle and scrub through which rocky, uncertain paths twisted and turned. Stunted oleanders grew here and there in no particular pattern on the edges of the piazza. There were no sidewalks. A handful of houses had dusty gardens alternating with large open spaces enclosed by chain-link fences. The houses looked tiny as they skirted the square, and the gaping sky over the immense rectangle only amplified the sense of abandonment and misery.

The boys crossed the piazza diagonally, walking two by two like monks. The last in line were Agostino and Tortima. Agostino was carrying two long skewers of mushrooms, and Tortima, in his big hands, a pair of sparrows with bleeding dangling heads.

As they reached the far side of the piazza, Tortima poked his elbow into Agostino's side. Pointing to one of the houses, he remarked cheerily, "Do you see that? Do you know what it is?"

Agostino took a look. It was a house very similar to the others. Maybe a little bigger, three stories high with a pitched roof covered by slate tiles. The front was painted a sad smoky gray with tightly closed white shutters, and it was almost completely hidden by the trees in the overgrown garden. The garden didn't appear to be very big. The perimeter wall was covered with ivy, and through the gate you could see a short driveway between two rows of bushes. Beneath an old awning was a door with closed shutters. "There's nobody home," said Agostino, pausing to get a better look.

"Nobody?" the other boy said, laughing. In a few words he explained to Agostino who exactly did live there. On previous occasions Agostino had heard the boys talking about such houses, inhabited by women who stayed indoors all day and all night, ready and willing to welcome anyone for a price, but this was the first time he had actually seen one. Tortima's words reawakened in him all the strangeness and astonishment he had felt the first time he had heard them mentioned. Back then he had hardly been able to believe the existence of such a singular community, the generous and indiscriminate dispenser of the love that to him appeared so difficult. Now the same disbelief made him turn his eyes toward that house as if to detect traces in its outside walls of the incredible life they guarded. By contrast to the fantastic image he had of its rooms, each illuminated by a female nude, the house looked singularly old and grim. "Really?" he said, feigning indifference, but his heart had started beating faster.

"Yes," said Tortima, "it's the most expensive one in town." He added the particulars of the prices, the number of women, the people who went there, and the amount of time you could stay. The information almost displeased Agostino, since it substituted mundane details for the vague barbaric image of these forbidden places he had formed earlier. Still, feigning a nonchalant tone of idle curiosity, he asked his companion many questions. Now that his initial surprise and agitation had passed, an idea with a stubborn and singular vitality formed in his mind. Tortima, who seemed well informed, provided all the clarification he wanted. And so, since night had fallen, the group broke apart amid the small talk. Agostino handed the mushrooms over to Tortima and headed home.

The idea had come to him, clear and simple, although its sources were complicated and obscure. That very evening, he would go to the house and know one of those women. It was not a desire or a yearning but rather a firm and almost desperate resolution.

Only in this way, he felt, would he finally succeed in freeing himself from the obsessions that had so tormented him during these summer days. Knowing one of those women, he thought vaguely, would forever discredit the boys' false accusations, and at the same time, sever once and for all the subtle bond of deviant and murky sensuality that had formed between the mother and himself. He couldn't admit it, but to feel finally released from that bond seemed the most urgent goal to be achieved. And he persuaded himself of its urgency no later than that same day through a very simple but significant development.

He and the mother had been sleeping in separate rooms, but that night a woman whom she had invited to spend a few weeks with them was supposed to arrive. Since the house was small, it had been decided that the guest would take Agostino's room while a cot would be set up for him in the mother's room. That same morning, before his displeased, scornful eyes, his cot had been placed next to the mother's bed, on which the sheets were heaped, still unmade and smelling of sleep. Along with the cot, his clothes, toiletries, and books had also been moved.

To see his already painful proximity to his mother increased by shared sleep filled Agostino with uncontrollable repulsion. All the things he had barely suspected till then, he thought, would suddenly be irremediably exposed to his eyes by virtue of this new and greater intimacy. As an antidote, he had to quickly, very quickly, insert between himself and his mother the image of another woman toward whom he could direct if not his gaze then at least his thoughts. This image—which would shield him from the mother's nudity and, in a way, strip her of all femininity, giving her back the motherly significance she had once held—could only be provided by one of the women in that house.

So how would he manage to penetrate and gain admission to that house? How should he behave in choosing the woman and retiring with her? None of this mattered to Agostino. Even if it had, he couldn't envision it. Because despite Tortima's accounts, the house, its inhabitants, and the things that happened inside it were still enveloped in a dense, improbable air, as if they involved not so much concrete realities as a series of hazardous guesses that, at the last minute, might even prove to be wrong. The success of his endeavor was thus confided to a logical calculation: If there was a house, there were also women; and if there were women, there was also the possibility of getting close to one of them. But he wasn't sure the house and the women really existed, and if they did, whether they resembled the image he had formed. It was not that he did not trust Tortima but rather that he had absolutely no terms of comparison. He had never done anything, never seen anything that had a thing in common, remotely or imperfectly, with what he was about to attempt. Like a poor savage who hears about the palaces of Europe and can only envision larger versions of his own hut, the only way he could imagine those women and their caresses was to think of his mother, so different and unimportant. The rest was daydreaming, fantasy, desire.

But as can happen, inexperience led him to dwell mainly on the practical aspects of the matter, as if, by settling them, he would also be able to solve the problem of how unrealistic the whole enterprise was. He was particularly worried by the question of money. Tortima had explained to him very carefully how much he would have to pay and to whom, but Agostino still could not wrap his mind around it. What was the relationship between money—which is generally needed to acquire clearly definable objects and verifiable quantities—and caresses, naked flesh, and the female body? How could a price be set on them, and how could such a price be calculated accurately and not vary each time? The idea of the money he would pay in exchange for that shameful, forbidden sweetness seemed strange and cruel, like an insult, which might be pleasurable to the person who delivers it but is painful to the one who receives it. Did he really have to pay the money directly to the woman or at least to someone in her presence? He felt it would be more appropriate for him to conceal the transaction from her, and leave her the illusion of a less interested relation. Finally, wasn't the sum indicated by Tortima too small? No amount of money, he thought, could pay for an experience such as the one he expected to conclude one period of his life and inaugurate another.

In the face of these doubts, he decided in the end to stick closely to Tortima's information. Even if untrue, it was nevertheless the only thing on which he could base a plan of action. He had persuaded a companion to tell him the price of a visit to the house, and the sum had seemed larger than the savings he had long been setting aside and keeping in a clay piggy bank. Between coins and small bills he must have scraped together the right amount and maybe even surpassed it. Maybe he could take the money from the piggy bank, wait until his mother had left to pick up her friend from the train station, go out himself, run to find Tortima, and then proceed to the house with him. Then the money would have to be enough for him and Tortima, whom he knew was poor as well as unwilling to do him any favors without receiving a personal benefit in return. This was the plan, and although he continued to see it as hopelessly remote and improbable, he decided to act on it with the same accuracy and certainty as a boat trip or a raid of the pine grove.

Excited, anxious, and for the first time free of the venom

of guilt and impotence, he ran almost the whole way, crossing the town from the piazza to his house. When he arrived the door was locked, but the shutters of the living-room window on the ground floor were open. Through the window he could hear piano music. He went in. His mother was sitting in front of the keyboard. The two soft lamps on the piano illuminated her face, leaving most of the room in darkness. She was sitting upright on a stool, playing the piano. Next to her, on another stool, was the young boatman. It was the first time Agostino had seen him in their house, and a sudden premonition took his breath away. His mother seemed to have noticed Agostino's presence, since she turned her head toward him with a calm and unconsciously flirtatious gesture. A flirtatiousness—to his mind, at least —directed more at the young man than at him, its supposed object. At the sight of him, she immediately stopped playing and asked him to draw nearer. "Agostino, is this any hour to return home? Come to me."

He slowly approached her, filled with repulsion and awkwardness. The mother pulled him close, wrapping an arm around his body. In her eyes Agostino could see an extraordinary brightness, a sparkling youthful fire. Her mouth seemed to be restraining a nervous laughter that coated her teeth with saliva. And in the act of wrapping her arm around him and pulling him to her side, he felt an impetuous violence and a trembling joyousness that almost frightened him. They were effusions, he could not help but think, that had nothing to do with him. Strangely they made him think of his own excitement a little earlier when he was running through the streets of the city, thrilled at the idea of taking his savings, going to the house with Tortima, and possessing a woman.

"Where have you been?" the mother continued in a tender, cruel, but cheerful voice. "Where have you been all this time? You're such a naughty boy." Agostino said nothing, in part because he had the impression his mother was not awaiting an answer. The same way, he thought to himself, she sometimes spoke to the cat. The young man looked at him and smiled, leaning forward, his hands clasped between his knees, a cigarette between two fingers, and his eyes sparkling just like the mother's. "Where have you been?" she repeated. "Naughty boy...you little rascal." With her big, long, warm hand, she ruffled his hair with a caress of tender and irresistible violence, and then smoothed it back down on his forehead. "He's such a handsome boy, isn't he?" she added proudly, turning toward the young man.

"Handsome like his mother," the young man replied. The mother laughed pathetically at this simple compliment. Agitated and filled with embarrassment, Agostino started to pull away. "Now go wash up," the mother told him, "and don't take all day. We're having dinner soon." Agostino said goodbye to the young man and left the room. From behind him, the musical notes resumed immediately, picking up where they had been interrupted by his entrance.

Once he was in the hall, he stopped and lingered to listen to the sounds the mother's fingers were releasing from the keyboard. The hall was dark and stuffy. At one end you could see, through the open door, the illuminated kitchen and the cook dressed in white busying herself slowly between the table and the stove. In the meantime the mother was playing, and to Agostino the music sounded lively, tumultuous, sparkling, in every way similar to the expression in her eyes when she was holding him close to her side.

Maybe it was the type of music, or maybe again it was the mother adding the tumult, the sparkle, and the liveliness. The whole house echoed with it, and Agostino found himself wondering whether outside in the street there might be clusters of people stopping to listen in amazement to the scandalous indiscretion resounding in each of those notes.

Then, all at once, midway through a chord, the sounds came to a stop. Agostino had a dark certainty that the force ringing through the music had suddenly found a more appropriate outlet. He took two steps back and set foot on the threshold of the living room.

What he saw did not greatly surprise him. The young man was standing up and kissing the woman on the mouth. Bent over backward on the low, narrow piano stool, which her body overflowed on every side, she still had one hand on the keyboard and the other wrapped around the young man's neck. In the dim light you could see her body twisted back, her palpitating breast exposed, one leg bent and the other extended to touch the pedal. In contrast to her violent devotion, the young man seemed to maintain his customary distance and composure. From his upright position, he had one arm under the woman's neck, more out of fear that she would fall, you might say, than out of violent passion. The other arm dangled to his side, the hand still holding a cigarette. His legs were clothed in white, sturdy and open, one on either side of her, expressing both self-possession and determination.

The kiss was long, and it seemed to Agostino that every time the young man wanted to break away, the mother would begin again with unsated greed. The truth was, he could not help thinking, she seemed starved for that kiss, like someone who has gone without for too long. Then, in a movement she made with her hand, one, two, three low and sweet notes were played in the living room. Instantly the two of them broke apart. Agostino took a step into the living room and said, "Mamma."

The young man turned around quickly and went to position himself, hands in his pockets, legs spread wide, by the window, as if he had been absorbed in looking out at the street. "Agostino," the mother said.

Agostino walked toward her. She was breathing with such violence he could clearly see her breasts rise and fall beneath the silk fabric of her dress. Her eyes were shining even more brightly than before. Her mouth was half open and her hair in disarray. A soft, pointed lock of hair, alive as a snake, cascaded down her cheek. "What is it, Agostino?" she repeated in a hoarse low voice, fixing her hair as best she could.

Agostino suddenly felt pity mixed with repulsion pressing down on his heart. "Get a hold of yourself," he wanted to shout at the mother, "calm down. Don't breathe like that. Then you can speak to me, but don't speak to me in that voice." Instead, quickly and almost deliberately exaggerating his childish voice and eagerness, he asked, "Mamma, can I break my piggy bank? I want to buy a book."

"Of course you can, dear," she said, and she reached out a hand as if to pat him on the forehead. As soon as her hand touched him, Agostino could not help but recoil, slightly and almost imperceptibly, but enough for it to seem violent and very noticeable to him. "OK, so I'll go ahead and break it," he repeated. And walking away quickly, without awaiting her reply, he left the room.

Running up steps that were squeaky with sand, he went to his room. The idea of the piggy bank hadn't been an excuse. He really hadn't known what to say at the sight of his overwrought mother. The piggy bank was on the desk at the far end of the dark room. Light from the streetlamp entered through the open window, illuminating its pink belly and wide black smile. Agostino switched on the light, grabbed the piggy bank, and with an almost hysterical violence threw it on the floor. The piggy bank broke and through a wide crack spewed a pile of coins of every type. Strewn in with the coins were several small bills. Squatting on the ground, Agostino counted the money in a fury. His fingers trembled, and although he was counting he couldn't help but see, mixed in with the coins scattered on the floor, the superimposed image of the two people in the living room, the mother tilted back on the stool and the young man leaning over her. He counted and sometimes he had to start over because of the confusion the image wrought in his mind. Once he had finished counting the money, he found he still didn't have the amount he required.

He wondered what he should do, and for a moment he thought of stealing the money from the mother. He knew where she kept it. Nothing would be easier, but the idea repelled him and he finally decided simply to ask her. What excuse should he use? Suddenly he thought he had found one. At the same time he heard the dinner bell tinkle. He quickly put his treasure in a drawer and went downstairs.

The mother was already seated at the dinner table. The window was open and from the courtyard big hairy brown moths came in and fluttered their wings against the white glass lampshade. The young man was gone, and the mother had regained her customary serene dignity. Agostino looked at her and once again, like the first time she had gone out to sea with the young boatman, he was surprised not to see on her mouth any trace of the kiss that just a few minutes earlier had pressed her lips together and then separated them. He couldn't say what he was feeling. A sense of compassion for his mother, to whom that kiss must have felt precious and overwhelming. And at the same time, a strong repulsion not at what he had seen but rather at the memory it had left. He would have preferred to reject the memory, to forget it. How could something so disturbing, so radical, enter through his eyes? He had a premonition the image would be impressed on his memory forever.

After they had finished eating, the mother stood up and went upstairs. Agostino thought the moment had come— it was now or never—to ask her for the money. He followed her and entered the bedroom behind her. She was sitting in front of the mirror at the vanity table and studying her face in silence.

"Mamma," said Agostino.

"What is it?" she asked absentmindedly.

"May I have twenty lire?" That was the amount he still needed.

"What for?"

"To buy a book."

"But didn't you say," she asked, slowly passing the powder puff over her face, "that you wanted to break your piggy bank?"

Agostino uttered a childish sentence. "Yes, but if I break it, then I won't have any money saved up. I want to buy the book without breaking the piggy bank."

The mother laughed affectionately. "You're such a child." She looked at him in the mirror for a moment, then added, "In my bag...on the bed, my change purse must be inside..."

you can take twenty lire and then put the purse back inside my bag."

Agostino went to the bed, opened the bag, removed the change purse, and took the twenty lire. Then, with the two bills in his fist, he threw himself on the cot prepared for him next to his mother's bed. The mother had finished retouching her makeup. She stood up from the vanity and came near him. "What are you going to do now?"

"I'm going to read this book," said Agostino, picking out at random an adventure novel from the bedside table and opening it to an illustration.

"Good boy, but remember to turn the light out before you fall asleep." She made a few more preparations, moving around the room. Lying down with one arm under his neck, Agostino glanced at her. The confused sensation came to him that she had never been as beautiful as she was that night. Her white dress of shimmering silk threw into stunning relief the warm brown color of her skin. By an unconscious blossoming of her former self, she appeared at that moment to have regained all the sweet and serene majesty of her former demeanor, but with something more, intangible, a deep sensual aura of happiness. She was big, but she looked bigger than Agostino had ever seen her, big enough to fill the whole room. A white glow in the shadowy bedroom, she moved majestically, her head held high on a beautiful neck, her black eyes tranquil, intent beneath her untroubled brow. She turned off all the lights except the one on the bedside table and bent down to kiss her son. Agostino once again felt enveloped by a perfume he knew intimately, and brushing his lips against her neck he could not help but wonder whether the women, back at that house, were as beautiful or as sweetly perfumed.

all women
compared to his mother

Left to himself, Agostino waited about ten minutes for the mother to be far enough away. Then he got out of bed, switched off the lamp, and tiptoed to the next room. He groped around the desk by the window, opened the drawer, and stuffed his pockets with the coins and bills. After he had finished, he searched the drawer, long and wide, to make sure he hadn't missed anything, and he left the room.

On the street he started running. Tortima lived on almost the opposite end of town, in a neighborhood of caulkers and sailors. Although the town was small, it was still quite a distance. He took dark roads near the pine grove, and walking quickly and occasionally breaking into a run, he went straight until he could see the masts popping up between the houses of the sailboats moored at the dock. Tortima's house was right on the dock, past the iron drawbridge that crossed the canal to the harbor. By day it was an old, rundown area, with rows of dilapidated houses and shops along wide, deserted, sunlit piers, the stench of fish and tar, green oil-slicked water, motionless cranes, and barges filled with rubble. But at this hour, the night made it look like all the other places in town, and only a large sailboat, looming over the sidewalks with all its sides and masts, revealed the presence of harbor waters deeply embanked between the houses. It was a long brown sailboat. High up, between the riggings, you could see the stars shining. The whole mast and hull seemed to be barely moving, in silence, with the ebb and flow of the canal. Agostino crossed the bridge and headed toward the row of houses on the opposite side of the canal. The occasional streetlamp cast an uneven light on the façades of the dilapidated houses. Agostino stopped beneath an open, illuminated window through which you could hear the sound of voices and dishes, of people eating. Bringing a hand to his mouth, he intoned a loud whistle followed by two softer ones, the signal agreed on by the boys in the gang. Almost immediately someone appeared at the window.

"It's me, Pisa," Agostino said in a low timorous voice.

"I'm coming," replied Tortima, for it was none other than him.

Tortima came outside with a face flushed by the wine he had drunk, still chewing on a morsel of something. "I came by so we could go to that house," said Agostino. "I've got the money here, enough for both of us." Tortima swallowed with a gulp and stared at him. "That house . . . on the far side of the piazza," Agostino repeated, "where the women are."

"Oh," said Tortima, finally understanding, "you had second thoughts. Good boy, Pisa. I'll be ready to come with you in a minute." He hurried off and Agostino stayed in the street, walking up and down, his eyes trained on Tortima's window. The older boy made him wait for a while and, when he reappeared, Agostino could hardly recognize him. He had always seen Tortima as an overgrown boy in rolled-up trousers, or half naked on the beach or in the water. Now he was gazing upon some young factory worker in his Sunday best, long pants and jacket, white collar, tie. He looked older also because of the pomade he had used to smooth his naturally curly hair. In his neat but plain clothes, he revealed to Agostino's eyes for the first time his qualities as a stolid city dweller.

"Let's get going," said Tortima, setting off.

"Is this the right time?" asked Agostino, running alongside him and crossing the iron bridge with him.

"It's always the right time there," replied Tortima with a smile.

They took different roads from the ones Agostino had followed on his way there. The square was not very far, barely two streets over. "Have you ever been there?" asked Agostino.

"Not to that one, no."

Tortima didn't seem to be in any hurry and moved at his usual pace. "Right now they've just finished eating and no one will be there," he explained. "It's the perfect time."

"Why?" asked Agostino.

"You have to ask? Because that way we can choose whoever we like."

"But how many are there?"

"Well, about four or five."

Agostino wanted to ask whether they were pretty but he kept his question to himself. "How are you supposed to act?" he asked. Tortima had already told him, but since he was still haunted by a sense of unreality he could not overcome, he needed to hear it reconfirmed.

"How are you supposed to act?" repeated Tortima. "It's easy. You go inside, then they introduce themselves. You say: Good evening, ladies. You pretend to make small talk for a while, just to give yourself enough time to have a good look around. Then you choose one. It's your first time, huh?"

"Well, actually—" Agostino began, somewhat embarrassed.

"Who do you think you're fooling?" said Tortima with brutality. "Don't think you can tell me this isn't your first time. Tell those fibs to other people, not to me. But don't worry," he added, with an odd emphasis.

"What do you mean?"

"Don't worry, I said. The woman knows what to do ... let her take care of it."

Agostino said nothing. The image conjured up by Tortima, of a woman who would introduce him to love, was pleasant and sweet and almost maternal. But despite this information, his disbelief persisted. "But...but...will they take me?" he asked, stopping and casting a glance at his own bare legs.

For a second the question seemed to embarrass Tortima. "Come on, let's get moving," he said with feigned indifference. "Once we're there, we'll find a way to get you in."

From a dirt road they came out into the piazza. The whole square was dark except a corner where a streetlamp illuminated with its tranquil light a large patch of rough sandy terrain. In the sky, right above the square, you might say, a crescent moon hung, smoky and red, cut in two by a thin wisp of fog. Where the darkness was deepest, Agostino spied the house, which he recognized from the white shutters. They were all closed tight and not a single ray of light shone through. Tortima headed toward the house confidently. But when they reached the middle of the square, beneath the crescent moon, he said to Agostino, "Give me the money. It's better if I keep it."

"But I—" Agostino started to say, not trusting Tortima.

"Are you going to give it to me or not?" Tortima insisted with brutality. Embarrassed that it was all in small change, Agostino obeyed him and emptied his pockets into his companion's hands. "Now keep quiet and follow me," Tortima said.

As they approached the house, the shadows grew softer, and the two gateposts, the driveway, and the doorway beneath the awning came into view. The gate was ajar. Tortima gave it a push and entered the yard. The door was also open a crack. Tortima climbed the steps and after making a

gesture to Agostino to keep quiet, he went in. Before Agostino's curious eyes appeared a small, completely bare entryway, at the far end of which a double door with red and blue
windowpanes glowed in the bright light. Their entrance
had set off a loud buzzer, and almost immediately a massive
shadow, like a seated person standing, was projected behind the glass and a woman appeared in the doorway. She
was some sort of maid, corpulent and older, with a large
bosom clothed in black and a white apron tied around her
waist. She came out belly-first, with her arms to her sides
and a bloated, grumpy, suspicious face beneath a knot of
hair. "Here we are," said Tortima. From his voice and demeanor, Agostino could tell that Tortima, usually so bold,
was also intimidated.

The woman gave them a long hard look, and then, in silence, beckoned to Tortima as if to invite him in. Tortima
smiled, relieved, and hurried toward the glass-paned door.
Agostino started to follow. "Not you," said the woman,
stopping him with a hand on his shoulder.

"What do you mean?" asked Agostino, suddenly losing
his timidity. "He can and I can't?"

"I really shouldn't let either of you in," said the woman,
staring at him, "but he gets in. You don't."

"You're too little, Pisa," said Tortima mockingly. And
with a push through the double door he disappeared. His
squat shadow appeared for a second behind the glass; then
it vanished into the bright light.

"But I—" Agostino insisted, exasperated by Tortima's
treachery.

"Get out of here, little boy. Go home," said the woman.
She went to the door, opened it, and found herself face-to-
face with two men on their way in. "Good evening, good

evening," said the first, a man with a ruddy, jovial face. "We have an agreement, right?" he added, turning to his companion, a pale thin blond. "If Pina is free, she's mine. I mean it."

"Agreed."

"What does this kid want?" asked the jovial man, pointing at Agostino.

"He wanted to get in," said the woman. A fawning smile was outlined on her lips.

"You wanted to get in?" the man shouted at Agostino. "You wanted to get in? At your age you should be home this hour of the night. Go home, go home," he shouted, waving his arms.

"That's what I told him," the woman replied.

"And if we let him in?" remarked the blond man. "At his age I was already making love to the maid."

"Who do you think you're fooling? Go home, go home!" shouted the man, infuriated. "Go home!" With the blond man right behind him, he burst through the door, slamming it behind him. Before he knew what had happened, Agostino found himself outside in the yard.

Everything had ended badly, he thought. Tortima had cheated him, taking the money, and he himself had been kicked out. Not knowing what to do, he walked backwards down the driveway, gazing at the half-open door, the awning, the front of the house rising before him with its white shutters closed tight. He felt a searing sense of disappointment, especially because of the way the two men had treated him, like a child. He found the jovial man's shouting and the blond's cold tentative kindness no less humiliating than the matron's blunt, expressionless hostility. Still walking backward, looking around and peering at the trees and bushes in the dark yard, he headed toward the gate. But he suddenly noticed that one whole part of the garden, on the left side of the house, appeared to be illuminated by a bright light that seemed to emanate from an open window on the ground floor. It occurred to him that through the window he would at least be able to get a glimpse of the house. Trying to make as little noise as possible, he worked his way toward the light.

As he imagined, it was a ground-floor window, wide open. The windowsill wasn't very high. Slowly but surely, hewing close to the corner where it was less likely he would be seen, he approached the window and peered inside.

The room was small and brightly lit. The walls were papered with a gaudy floral pattern in green and black. Opposite the window, a red curtain, hanging by wooden rings from a brass rod, seemed to conceal a door. There was no furniture. Someone was sitting in a corner, on the window side. All you could see were his crossed feet in yellow shoes extended almost to the middle of the room: the feet, Agostino thought, of a man comfortably settled in an armchair. Disappointed, he was about to withdraw when the curtain was lifted and a woman appeared.

She was wearing a loose sheer sky-blue gown that reminded Agostino of his mother's negligees. The gown, transparent, reached all the way down to her feet. Beneath the sheer material, the woman's limbs, which took on the aquamarine tint of the fabric, appeared pale and long, almost swaying in lazy curves around the dark stain of her pelvis. Her gown, in a bizarre detail that impressed Agostino, parted over her chest in an oval neckline that dipped all the way down to her waist. Her breasts, which were round and heavy, protruded almost painfully, naked and tightly squeezed against each other. Her gown, which surrounded her breasts with a tightly pleated frame, then reconnected at the neck. Her wavy brown hair was loose and tumbled to her shoulders. She had a wide face, flat and pale, like a spoiled child, and a whimsical expression in her weary eyes and on the pursed lips of her painted mouth. With her hands behind her back and her breasts out, she emerged through the curtain and for a long moment, in an expectant pose, she stood straight and still, without saying a word. She seemed to be looking toward the corner at the man whose crossed feet could be seen in the middle of the room. Then, in the same silence with which she had come, she turned around, lifted the curtain, and disappeared. Almost immediately the man's feet retreated from Agostino's view. There was the sound of someone standing up. Frightened, Agostino drew away from the window.

He returned to the driveway, gave a shove to the gate, and went out into the piazza. He was feeling a strong sense of disappointment over his failed venture. At the same time he was gripped almost by terror at what awaited him in the days to come. Nothing had happened, he thought. He hadn't been able to possess a single woman. Tortima had taken his money, and the next day the teasing of the boys and the impure torment of his relations with his mother would resume. It's true that for a moment he had seen the woman he desired, standing in her sheer gown, her breasts naked. But he had a dark sense that this inadequate and ambiguous image would be the only picture of womanhood to accompany his memories for long years to come. In fact, years and years would go by, empty and unhappy, between him and the liberating experience. Not until he was as old as Tortima, he thought, would he be released once and for all from this awkward age of transition. But in the meantime he had to continue living in the same way. He felt his whole spirit rebel against the thought, like the bitter sense of a final impossibility.

Once he reached home, he entered without making a sound. In the doorway he saw the guest's suitcases and heard voices in the living room. Then he climbed the stairs and went to throw himself on the cot in his mother's bedroom. There, in the dark, angrily tearing off his clothes and tossing them on the ground, he got undressed and slipped under the sheets. Then he waited, his eyes wide open in the blackness.

He waited a long while. At a certain point he started to feel drowsy and he really did nod off. All at once he woke with a start. The lamp was on, illuminating the mother's back. She was wearing a negligee and had one knee on the bed, getting ready to turn in for the night. "Mamma," he said immediately in a loud and almost violent voice.

The mother turned around and came near him. "What's wrong?" she asked. "Is something the matter, dear?" Her negligee was transparent, like the gown of the woman at the house. Her body was also shaped like the other body, in vague lines and shadows. "I want to leave tomorrow," said Agostino, in the same loud and exasperated voice, trying not to look at the mother's body but at her face.

The mother, startled, sat down on the bed and stared at him. "Why? What's the matter? Aren't you having a good time here?"

"I want to leave tomorrow," he repeated.

"We'll see," said the mother, discreetly passing a hand over his forehead, as if she was afraid he had a fever. "What's the matter? Don't you feel well? Why do you want to leave?"

Agostino said nothing. The mother's negligee reminded him of the gown worn by the woman at the house, the same transparency, the same pale flesh, listless and within reach. Except the negligee was wrinkled, making it even more intimate and his glimpse of her even more furtive. So, Agostino thought, not only did the image of the woman at the house not act as a screen between himself and the mother, as he had hoped, but it had somehow confirmed the mother's womanhood. "Why do you want to leave?" she asked again. "Don't you enjoy spending time with me?"

"You always treat me like a baby," Agostino said all at once, not even he knew why.

The mother laughed and patted him on the cheek. "All right, then, from now on I'll treat you like a man. Will that make you happy? Now go to sleep...it's late." She bent down and kissed him. With the light out, Agostino could hear her getting into bed.

"Like a man," he couldn't help but think to himself before falling asleep. But he wasn't a man, and many unhappy days would pass before he became one.

TRANSLATOR'S NOTE

In the book-length interview he granted to his friend, the writer Alain Elkann, Alberto Moravia described *Agostino* as "the hinge that connects *Gli indifferenti* with my later works." Written in one month in 1942 on the island of Capri, the novel marked a return to form both in his own and in critical estimation. He felt that it recaptured the "spontaneous, necessary quality" that had characterized his debut novel, *Gli indifferenti* (translated as *The Time of Indifference*), whose success had initially proved difficult to repeat. Published in 1929 when Moravia was twenty-one years old, the novel was reprinted four times before it came out in a second edition in 1934. By contrast his next long novel, *Le ambizioni sbagliate* (*The Mistaken Ambitions*, 1935), on which he had labored for seven years, was a disappointment, aggravated by the censorship of the Fascist regime, which instructed the newspapers not to review the novel and confiscated his next, *La mascherata* (*The Fancy Dress Party*, 1941).

Agostino was first published by a smaller house, Documento, in 1943 and then brought out in a revised edition the next year by Bompiani. In 1945 it was awarded Italy's first postwar literary prize, the Corriere Lombardo. It is indeed a "hinge" or transitional work, certainly in terms of his career: the publication of *La romana* (*The Woman of*

Rome) two years later would establish his international reputation, and his works began to appear in translation. The themes of *Agostino* indicate a broadening of the author's focus—although his gaze remains resolutely centered on the bourgeoisie—and a deeper engagement with the themes of poverty and social injustice. In his conversations with Elkann, Moravia described the work as "the story of a childhood vacation, but . . . also the story of Agostino's encounter with modern culture, and its premise is the work of two great unmaskers, Marx and Freud." While his interest in Freudian psychology was already apparent in *Gli indifferenti*, his exploration of class conflict heralds a new era in his writing as part of the general movement in Italian culture known as neorealism. Moravia collaborated closely with the most important postwar film directors, and many of his works, most prominently *La ciociara* (translated into English as *Two Women*), were adapted for the big screen.

But it is the stylistic transition in *Agostino* that most interests me as a translator. Although he tired of the attention it garnered, Moravia's prose stood out from the beginning as spare and brutal, especially by comparison to the high literary manner that prevailed in Italy during the early years of the century. His champions and critics alike pointed to what they considered his unadorned style. In one of the first reviews of *Gli indifferenti*, the novelist Giuseppe Antonio Borgese praised Moravia as having "a very beautiful art of writing because it is cleansed of frills, the exact opposite of the vexing lack of originality, the false and toxic 'beautiful writing,' that had reduced prose to tattoos with acid." These same features were dismissed by more traditional critics, most famously the great philologist Gianfranco Contini, who called Moravia's prose "a gray and neutral koiné of the capital city, the zero-degree language of a Pirandello stripped of gesture."

Contini and others acted as gatekeepers of a literary tradition rooted in the courtly love poetry of thirteenth- and fourteenth-century Tuscany. Its strictures were such, in the most extreme instances of the Renaissance, that not a single word could be used that was not found in Petrarch or Boccaccio. In as linguistically fragmented a country as Italy, with its many regional and even local dialects, writing in "pure" standard Italian was a daunting challenge for writers from outside the Florence–Rome matrix. For the modern novelist, starting with Manzoni, the challenge was to transform an essentially lyric medium into a flexible, contemporary prose adapted to the needs of narrative realism.

In a recent book-length study of Moravia's style, Gianluca Lauta documents the more conventional aspect of his prose as well as its distinctiveness. He argues that the often criticized blandness of Moravia's dialogues is shaped by the intellectual emptiness of his bourgeois characters: "On the one hand, *Gli indifferenti* participates in the collapse of the grand classical style, on the other, it comes close to the superficial dialogues, typical of salons, that had been used in lowbrow novels for at least two centuries." Comparing the edits that Moravia made from the first to the second editions of *Agostino*, Lauta notes his "clear intention to use the most appropriate word, even to the detriment of perfectly acceptable forms."

The idea that Moravia was engaged in "invisible writing" or tearing down the edifice of classical Italian is not entirely borne out by a close analysis of *Agostino*. I would say instead that he is turning the literary tradition on its head, adopting the conventions of courtly love poetry but for more earthly ends. Like many a forlorn poet, the narrator suffers the afflictions of unrequited love, but the object of his affection, scandalously, is his mother. Rather than seek to elevate her, like Petrarch's Laura, he is intent on debasing her, repeating, like a mantra, "She's only a woman." In his eyes her body takes on distorted proportions, and exudes, after her indiscretions with the young boatman, an "acrid, violent animal warmth."

Moravia drives home the clash between the language he has inherited and the reality he is depicting through other borrowings from Renaissance poetry. The mother is often presented as "wrapped" in an air, an article of clothing, or even the sheets, heightening her inaccessibility. Agostino's fetishistic evocation of her clothing—the wet bathing suit pressed against his cheek, the negligee in which she stands before her mirror—is the inverse image of the courtier's attachment to his beloved's veil, glove, or handkerchief. And in words that evoke this same tradition, Moravia uses the adjective *antico*—which today signifies "ancient" or "old" but archaically meant "former"—to describe the mother's lost dignity and the son's lost innocence.

The obsessive, even grating repetition of certain words and phrases is rooted, I believe, in the same subversive impulse. It was Moravia's severe critic, Contini, who coined the expression "monolinguism" to define Petrarch's paring down of poetic language to a few rarefied terms. Moravia's select vocabulary is of another and indeed opposite nature. Agostino is torn between feelings of "attraction" and "repulsion." His confused, in-between state is captured by another frequent word, "murky" (*torbido*), with strange and visceral undertones. The sexual goings-on that Agostino is slowly becoming aware of are *oscuri* (dark, mysterious, or obscure), denoting, in simplified form, the Freudian unconscious. The only way out of his confusion, he is convinced, is to become a man, a wish he voices in a dreamlike state at the beginning and the end of the novel.

These repetitions forge disquieting links between the characters. The mother's "awkwardness" is echoed in the ungainliness of the boys. The image of the sheer negligee on the prostitute at the brothel is superimposed on the wrinkled nightgown the mother is wearing when she comforts Agostino. The bluntness of these parallels, combined with the word pictures Moravia creates of the mother before the mirror, the boat on the sea, or the stream through the canebrake, suggest a painterly technique. He observes visual detail like a portrait artist. Take the passage where Agostino spies on his mother from behind the door:

> The mother, having removed her necklace and set it on the marble top of the chest of drawers, brought her hands together at her earlobe in a graceful gesture to unscrew one of the earrings. Throughout this motion, she kept her head tilted to one side and turned toward the room.

Or the gang of boys as they prepare to go skinny-dipping:

> Against the green background of the cane, their bodies were brown and white, a miserable, hairy white from their groins to their bellies. This whiteness revealed something strangely deformed, ungainly, and overly muscular about their bodies, typical of manual laborers.

The bluntness of his repetitions, on the other hand, reminds me of the bold outlines that were popular in the social realist paintings of postwar Italy, particularly in the work of Renato Guttuso. Guttuso was in fact a close friend of Moravia's and painted two portraits of the novelist. He also illustrated the Bompiani edition of *Agostino*.

In translating the novel I have tried to preserve the repetitions, though it has not always been possible, especially the adjective "obscure," whose many nuances no single word could seem to capture. A particularly vexing issue was how to refer to the boat that figures so largely in the story, the *pattino*, not to mention the structure of Italian beach culture in general, both then and now. A *pattino*, also known as a *moscone*, looks like a paddle boat but is propelled by oars rather than foot pedals, and is used not only for sunbathing but also by lifeguards to rescue people.

For the central figure of the mother, the Italian language has an ambiguous expression, *la madre*, which could be translated as either "his mother" or "the mother." I generally opted for the later, in keeping with the archetypal importance she assumes in Agostino's eyes, using "his mother" only where the Italian was more explicit or greater intimacy was suggested. The little black boy, Homs, is referred to throughout as *il moro*, "the Moor," which in erudite Italian can be used for a person of African origin (or a dark-haired male). To avoid introducing a note of linguistic violence not present in the original, I chose to refer to the character mostly by his name.

In closing, I would be remiss not to mention the previous translation of *Agostino* by Beryl de Zoete (Secker and Warburg, 1947). Once I had completed my first draft, I compared the more troubling parts against her earlier version. Where our divergences were too great, I went back to the Italian. On the whole, her work is very beautiful, perhaps too beautiful, often smoothing out edges Moravia had left rough, and with an occasional misinterpretation. She seems to shy away from the more coarse passages, reluctant, for instance, to translate the pubic hairs sprouting from Sandro's groin. The first chapter, oddly, is divided in two. Without being privy to the correspondence between the translator and the editor—and who knows, perhaps the multilingual Moravia himself also weighed in—it is hard to know who is responsible for these decisions.

—MICHAEL F. MOORE

REFERENCES

Giuseppe Antonelli. "La Scrittura invisibile." Alberto Moravia 2007. A cento anni dalla nascita. (http://www.uninettuno. tv/Video.aspx?v=129)

Gianfranco Contini. *Letteratura dell'Italia unita 1861–1968*. Firenze: Sansoni, 1994.

Louis Kibler. "Moravia and Guttuso: À la recherche de la réalité perdue." *Italica* 56, 2 (Summer 1979), 198–212.

Gianluca Lauta. *La scrittura di Moravia: lingua e stile dagli* Indifferenti *ai* Racconti romani. Milano: Franco Angeli, 2005.

Alberto Moravia and Alain Elkann. *Life of Moravia*. Translated by William Weaver. South Royalton, VT: Steerforth Italia, 2000.

Eileen Romano. "Cronologia," in *Agostino*. Alberto Moravia. Milano: Tascabili Bompiani, 2009.

TITLES IN SERIES

For a complete list of titles, visit www.nyrb.com or write to:
Catalog Requests, NYRB, 435 Hudson Street, New York, NY 10014

* *Also available as an electronic book.*

WILLIAM H. GASS On Being Blue: A Philosophical Inquiry*
THÉOPHILE GAUTIER My Fantoms
JEAN GENET Prisoner of Love
ÉLISABETH GILLE The Mirador: Dreamed Memories of Irène Némirovsky by Her Daughter*
JOHN GLASSCO Memoirs of Montparnasse*
P.V. GLOB The Bog People: Iron-Age Man Preserved
NIKOLAI GOGOL Dead Souls*
EDMOND AND JULES DE GONCOURT Pages from the Goncourt Journals
PAUL GOODMAN Growing Up Absurd: Problems of Youth in the Organized Society*
EDWARD GOREY (EDITOR) The Haunted Looking Glass
JEREMIAS GOTTHELF The Black Spider*
A.C. GRAHAM Poems of the Late T'ang
WILLIAM LINDSAY GRESHAM Nightmare Alley*
EMMETT GROGAN Ringolevio: A Life Played for Keeps
VASILY GROSSMAN An Armenian Sketchbook*
VASILY GROSSMAN Everything Flows*
VASILY GROSSMAN Life and Fate*
VASILY GROSSMAN The Road*
OAKLEY HALL Warlock
PATRICK HAMILTON The Slaves of Solitude
PATRICK HAMILTON Twenty Thousand Streets Under the Sky
PETER HANDKE Short Letter, Long Farewell
PETER HANDKE Slow Homecoming
ELIZABETH HARDWICK The New York Stories of Elizabeth Hardwick*
ELIZABETH HARDWICK Seduction and Betrayal*
ELIZABETH HARDWICK Sleepless Nights*
L.P. HARTLEY Eustace and Hilda: A Trilogy*
L.P. HARTLEY The Go-Between*
NATHANIEL HAWTHORNE Twenty Days with Julian & Little Bunny by Papa
ALFRED HAYES In Love*
ALFRED HAYES My Face for the World to See*
PAUL HAZARD The Crisis of the European Mind: 1680–1715*
GILBERT HIGHET Poets in a Landscape
RUSSELL HOBAN Turtle Diary*
JANET HOBHOUSE The Furies
HUGO VON HOFMANNSTHAL The Lord Chandos Letter*
JAMES HOGG The Private Memoirs and Confessions of a Justified Sinner
RICHARD HOLMES Shelley: The Pursuit*
ALISTAIR HORNE A Savage War of Peace: Algeria 1954–1962*
GEOFFREY HOUSEHOLD Rogue Male*
WILLIAM DEAN HOWELLS Indian Summer
BOHUMIL HRABAL Dancing Lessons for the Advanced in Age*
DOROTHY B. HUGHES The Expendable Man*
RICHARD HUGHES A High Wind in Jamaica*
RICHARD HUGHES In Hazard*
RICHARD HUGHES The Fox in the Attic (The Human Predicament, Vol. 1)*
RICHARD HUGHES The Wooden Shepherdess (The Human Predicament, Vol. 2)*
INTIZAR HUSAIN Basti*
MAUDE HUTCHINS Victorine
YASUSHI INOUE Tun-huang*
HENRY JAMES The Ivory Tower
HENRY JAMES The New York Stories of Henry James*